MW01128938

Play With Me

Eliza Gayle

DEDICATION

As always, thank you so much to my family
for all their support and understanding for the
time it takes to write the books I love.

OTHER BOOKS BY AUTHOR

SERIES

Pleasure Playground
PLAY WITH ME
POWER PLAY

Purgatory Masters
TUCKER'S FALL
LEVI'S ULTIMATUM

Purgatory Club
ROPED
DISPLAYED
WHIPPED
BURNED
BOTTOMS UP
FETISH DREAMS *print compilation*

What Alex Wants
SWEET SUBMISSION
RECLAIMING HIS SUBMISSIVE

Southern Shifters
LUCAS
KANE
MALCOLM
BAD KITTY
BE WERE
FROST BITTEN

Pentacles of Magick
UNTAMED MAGICK
MAGICK IGNITED
FORCE OF MAGICK
MAGICK PROVOKED
BOUND BY MAGICK *print compilation*

SINGLE TITLES

SUBMISSIVE BEAUTY
VAMPIRE AWAKENING
THE BILLIONAIRE'S DEMON
SLAVE TO PLEASURE
WICKED CHRISTMAS EVE
SUBMISSIVE SECRETS

ONE

Becoming a Peeping Tom had not been part of Eve Blake's job description when she took the receptionist position at Altered Ego. Yet that's exactly what she'd become. She'd thought working for a fetish photographer might help her get out of the shell she'd been hiding in, but this was ridiculous.

Eve stood in the dressing room, staring at the thin white curtain that hid the main photo studio from her view. Her nipples tightened just thinking about what she'd see. When today's model had arrived, she'd confirmed on the schedule that Chase and Murphy had booked Jennifer for one of the hard-core assignments. All three had disappeared into the studio hours ago, and the urge to witness what happened behind the curtain drove her back here.

Unfortunately, this watching had become a habit.

The studio, depending on the props and lighting Chase used, could be transformed from a lush den of seduction to a full-on BDSM dungeon. Today would be the dungeon.

In the interest of full disclosure, Chase had been up-front with her from the beginning. He shot photos of any and all types of sensual fantasies, from what some labeled erotic art, all the way to what many classified as porn. She'd seen some of those pictures, and on one level they were explicit beyond belief, and on another the most tantalizing sexuality she'd laid eyes on. Sometimes when she studied them, she'd grow jealous of the models and long to be in their position. Especially the photos that included Murphy.

Eve shuddered at the fresh wave of arousal flooding her sex. Everything about this place had turned her into a needy, "desperate to be fucked" woman. No, that wasn't quite right. It was more than simply being fucked. Sex was easy, and if all she wanted was to have some guy shove his dick in her, it would be easy enough to find. No, what Chase and Murphy did to a woman went far and above plain old sex.

They demanded. They manipulated. And they took whatever they wanted when they wanted.

What would it be like to be helpless under their control? Sure, both Chase and Murphy were professionals and much of what they did wasn't done for personal pleasure. Yet models begged for more jobs, and it wasn't exactly a secret when Chase or Murphy dated one of the girls. Dating being a very loose description of what they actually did with them.

The knots in Eve's stomach tightened further, and the flesh between her legs ached to be touched. She couldn't take the anticipation another second. She had to see for herself what lay behind the curtain.

She reached up and brushed the flimsy fabric a few inches aside and peered inside the darkened room. With the only wash of light in the large dungeon space spotlighted in the center of the room, Eve's gaze was automatically drawn to the two people in the midst of a scene. Jennifer, the skinny blonde model who'd arrived earlier, had been stripped of clothing except for red thigh-high latex stockings and red shoulder-length latex gloves. The bright color contrasted strongly with her oh-so-pale skin and nearly white hair, striking Eve with the sheer beauty of the woman.

The model's arms were pulled behind her body and tied at the wrists with a matching dyed rope, which was strung through a hook in the ceiling, stretching and suspending her arms behind her. Around her waist and thighs, they'd roped her with a simple harness and attached the rope to another hook in the dungeon wall at the back of the room.

In this position she could move quite a bit from left to right, but moving forward would be impossible. Jennifer's large breasts were bare and her shaved pussy completely visible as she stood with her legs spread wide.

Chase had explained their specialty in bondage, and every time she watched them tie a woman, it damned near drove her insane. Eve wanted to know everything. Did the rough rope abrading the skin hurt? Or was it a sensation that aroused a woman? Did the knowledge of being tied and helpless fuck with your mind? Or did knowing that Chase and Murphy had complete control to do whatever they wanted excite them? She'd bet her entire paycheck every model they touched wanted them.

A few feet in front of the model, Murphy stood wearing only black leather pants and combat boots. With his back to Eve, she got a good look at the tattoos that covered his skin. The tribal markings were inked in solid black in a series of swinging arcs and powerful curves. She had no idea of their meanings, if there were any, but they struck her as powerful and dominating. Especially when he moved.

Fascinated by the soft light glowing on his tanned skin, she barely noticed him move forward. The room they were in had been soundproofed, so unless Jennifer started really screaming, Eve would never hear a sound they made. It was easy to see why Chase used Murphy for his male model. With his midnight black hair and dark eyes that seemed to see clear through to a person's soul, there wasn't a woman alive who didn't respond to the aura of power that surrounded him. The thick muscles that flexed and bunched in every pose didn't hurt either.

A few minutes later Murphy moved from in front of Jennifer, and Chase and his camera took up his place. Chase's tousled brown hair stood on end, shooting in every direction. She easily pictured him pushing his hands through it in between shots, while he waited impatiently for Murphy to set up the next scene. His hard-to-read emerald eyes would be focused through the lens, and even though she couldn't see them, she imagined the heavily lashed, hooded gaze staring at her with lascivious intent. Never before meeting Chase had she really understood the phrase "bedroom eyes."

She'd admired the erotic portraits hung around the studio and reception area, and she'd scoured Chase's Web site, studying each and every picture. The sensuality he captured through a camera lens took her breath away every time until she'd begun to fantasize herself as one of his models.

Eve caught the flash of silver out of the corner of her eye and turned her head to investigate. Murphy had apparently attached huge clover clamps to Jennifer's breasts, and a heavy chain dangled between them. The heat and arousal she spied in the model's eyes could not be faked. She clearly enjoyed the pain of having her nipples clamped.

Curious, Eve unbuttoned her own blouse and pushed her bra out of the way, baring her sensitive tips to the cool air of the dressing room. Already tight from arousal, they went positively rock hard when she touched them. But it was the pain of a clamp she wanted to feel. So with two fingers of each hand she pinched tight, first absorbing the pressure and then letting it edge into a stronger bite. When she thought she'd hit the limit of what she could take, she squeezed harder until she took her own breath away.

Keeping the pressure steady, she watched Chase move around Jennifer, taking a series of pictures. She moved and swayed each time he spoke to her, and Eve imagined him barking out directions. He tended to get lost in his work sometimes and had no idea the effect his demanding tone had on a woman. Or maybe he did.

Eve had sat at her desk many times, taking orders from Chase and praying she wouldn't embarrass herself by having an orgasm from his voice alone. She shook her head at her ridiculous thoughts. Her reactions to him made her crazy. How could anyone sane be so influenced by a little thing like a man's voice? Her boss would probably be appalled if he ever got clued in to her thoughts.

Through the glass she saw Murphy move forward again, this time standing in a position that gave her a clear view to the model and him. He reached for the dangling chain and the model's mouth formed a little O. Jennifer's eyes widened as Eve imagined Murphy told her what he was about to do. He tugged on the chain and she scooted forward scant inches before the ropes that held her stopped her movement.

A smug smile crossed Murphy's face, and he pulled hard on that chain. Jennifer tried to move her arms, but she had nowhere to go. Her breasts stretched, she flung her head back and her mouth opened wide on a long scream Eve heard clearly through the glass. Her own fingers pulled, and heat rushed through her, making her breasts tingle and her thighs ache.

For a few precious seconds, she squeezed her eyes shut tight and reveled in the ecstasy building inside her. When she finally blinked her eyes open, Murphy had picked up a small black whip and moved behind Jennifer. He spoke to the woman and she nodded, leaving Eve to wish she could hear them as well as see them. Was he coaxing her through the shoot with reassurances, or did the scene take on a more realistic tone with commands any Dom would issue a submissive?

Either way, when he flicked his wrist and the small tail of the whip hit her backside, Jennifer's entire body jerked against the restraints and her face registered shock. All of course captured by Chase's camera. Murphy swung again and again, and Eve stood mesmerized by the facial expressions of the model. If she wasn't really into what they were doing, then she should be an actress, because the pain and pleasure she experienced was written all over her face.

Chase picked up the chain between her breasts and tugged while Murphy continued to whip her. The bulge at the front of his jeans made it clear how turned on he'd become by the beautiful submissive as the scene progressed. Eve's own panties had soaked through, and she longed to remove them. Releasing her grip from one of her nipples, Eve slid her hand down her rounded stomach and into the waistband of her silk underwear. Moisture clung to the small patch of hair covering her sex, and the first glancing touch across her swollen clit made her legs tremble with need.

Everything logical in her mind said the scene in front of her should offend her, but clearly her body had ideas of its own. Suddenly the desire to be the one tied and standing helpless between Murphy and Chase consumed her faster than a flame to dry timber. She plunged two fingers between her drenched folds and into her wanting sex. Rough and fast, that's what she wanted right now. God, how she needed more than fingers to fill her. Still, even at her own hand the visual of Chase and Murphy torturing the blonde beauty became too much.

She continued to thrust her fingers as the knot in her lower abdomen wound tight. She hovered on the precipice of release.

A sudden shrill ring sounded in her ear, and Eve froze in place.

An incoming call.

Fuck. Fuck. Fuck.

She had to take this. The phone rang in every room of the studio, and she had no idea whether Chase had turned his ringer off. She slid to the side, out of the window, and gulped for air. Her breathing had grown erratic, and a caller would not think her normal at the moment. After three rings she had no choice — either take the call or her ass would be grass when Chase finished his shoot. And in this economy she couldn't afford to lose her only job.

She tapped the earpiece and said, "Altered Ego. This is Eve. How may I help you?" She cringed at the breathless tone of her voice while she slowly moved from the dressing area and in the direction of the restroom. She squinted against the bright lights after being in the darkness, making her way mostly by memory.

"I'd like to speak with Chase Miller," a snide female voice demanded.

"He's in the middle of a shoot and unavailable for calls. I could either take a message, or if there is anything I can help with…" She hoped not. She could barely talk as it was. Eve pushed into the bathroom and locked the door behind her. She doubted anyone would be coming out of the studio anytime soon, but you never knew.

"I have a custom order for him. An urgent one."

"No problem. I can take the basic details and then send you the art form to be filled out. Although I'm not sure of Mr. Miller's availability. I will have to consult with him."

"No, no, it must be right away, but I'm certain once he finds out who his client will be, it won't be a problem." The over confident assistant annoyed her. A sure trait of the rich and famous and the select few who work for them.

"Okay. Then if you'd like to download the form from modelmayhem.com and submit it, I can be sure that Mr. Miller gets it as soon as he's finished with his current session." The loud sigh in her ear had Eve rolling her eyes.

"Fine. I will do that now and will expect a call back this afternoon, the moment Mr. Miller is free."

"Sure, no problem." The caller disconnected, and Eve pressed her earpiece to off.

Standing in front of the sink and mirror of the opulent bathroom Chase provided, she leaned heavily on her hands and gulped for air. A glance into the mirror was a stark reminder of exactly what she'd been up to. Her blouse was unbuttoned with her bra still pushed above her breasts, and her skirt sat bunched up around her waist. Thank God no one had walked into the receptionist area while she'd been peeping, or they'd have gotten an interesting eyeful when she'd answered the phone. Not like anyone familiar with Chase's fetish work would probably blink an eye though. A half-dressed woman around the studio was hardly uncommon.

She quickly washed her hands and put her clothes back to rights. But her hair had somehow become a disaster. She'd started to sweat, so some of it had plastered to the side of her face, and the rest reminded her of her morning bed head mess. She grabbed the makeup bag she left on the shelf and pulled out a brush and lipstick.

Having long hair came with a lot of work, but she felt that the red tresses were her best feature. Her friends often complimented her on it, along with the remark that if she'd just shed some of her weight, she'd be stunning. Eve stood back and studied her hips and thighs. Yes, she would never be called skinny, but she rather liked her curves.

Why did everyone have to be so obsessed with being tiny? What the hell was wrong with healthy? Not every man was looking for thin model types. She hoped anyway. With a small shrug, she hurried out of the bathroom. Not something she had time to worry about at the moment.

At her desk, she swiveled toward the computer and hit the button to bring up her e-mail, but her mind drifted back to the studio and the scene still going on. She never got to see the full details on most of the hard-core orders because Chase held them strictly confidential, but after what little she'd witnessed, her imagination had gone into overdrive. How far would they go? Did a custom order include fucking? The image of Murphy sliding his thick cock into Jennifer filled Eve's mind, and a groan slid from her mouth, which she quickly smothered with her hand.

Get it together before you find yourself in more trouble than you can handle.

Eve's e-mail popped up, and she took the distraction for what it was and scrolled through some of the junk to delete what she didn't need. The rest she filed to look at later when her brain wasn't mush. A new e-mail from the Web site popped open, and the subject line read:

Urgent Custom Order

No doubt from the caller who'd hung up on her a mere five minutes ago.

Curious, she clicked it open to find out more. As she expected, the order stated it came from a Mr. Smith. It wasn't uncommon for some of Chase's clients not to divulge their names on their paperwork. In those instances, he would take their private information directly. She scrolled through the particulars such as time of delivery, type of film, settings, and on down to the model information.

Model must be redheaded and of a plus-size nature with full breasts.

Eve nearly choked on her sip of coffee. In all the orders she'd taken, no one had ever asked for a plus-size model. Whoever the mystery customer was, she already liked him. A larger woman would be a refreshing change around here. She clicked to forward the message to Chase and went back to the rest of her e-mails. If she focused on her work, maybe she'd be able to get her mind off the scene she'd spied on at least long enough to get through the rest of the day.

When she got home, all bets were off, and her vibrator would get the workout of its life. A wicked smile tugged at her lips. She desperately wanted to know more about Chase and Murphy's private lives. Sure she knew a lot about their fetishes, but how deep into the BDSM scene did they go? Her pathetic and limited experience left her a little green, but mostly because she found it difficult to define her own needs, let alone find a Dom to click with.

So much of the local scene seemed to revolve around playing roles. Master and slave. Simply thinking the words made her muscles clench with excitement. Maybe one day she'd figure it out…understand how to be what a master sought.

"Eve."

She jumped at the sound of her name spoken in an attention getting tone. So lost in her thoughts she'd not heard Chase approach her desk. Her breath quickened and her pulse sped up from the one simple word. She lifted her lashes and looked at him through hooded eyes she prayed didn't look guilty. Because right now she felt like a naughty girl who'd just been busted. Thank God she'd refrained from touching herself again.

"This new order. Did you talk to them when they called?"

She nodded, too nervous to speak out loud yet. Mesmerized by the shade of green reflected in his gaze. In his case, eyes weren't windows to the soul. They were the microscope that saw into her thoughts. As if somehow he'd noticed her spying on him, or that the moment he said her name, renewed arousal dampened her panties, and he damned well knew it.

"Did they say who this was for?"

"No, but I did get the impression it was for someone pretty important. The woman was quite confident that you'd be willing to fill this order as quickly as they wanted." She tried not to fidget, but it was impossible to sit still with him looking at her with such intensity.

"That's too bad because as intriguing as this shoot would be, I'm going to have to turn this one down."

Damn. Even the tight frown of his lips turned her on. She'd give anything to trace the shape of his mouth, to explore every line.

"Why?"

"No model that fits the requirements. It's often hard enough to find a redhead for a hard-core shoot. But a plus-size model? No way. Not on this short of notice."

"What about me? I could do it." Eve clamped her hand over her mouth, shocked she'd blurted the offer out loud. Still, she'd made the offer, and she held her breath waiting for his response.

His eyes narrowed and he stared into her gaze. Searching for something maybe. Her neck warmed with the humiliation that crept through her.

"Come here," he demanded gruffly.

Worried, she moved from behind the reception desk and stood in front of him. Not squirming while he looked at her from head to toe proved impossible as she shifted from one foot to the other. He went back to staring into her eyes and she found it nerve-racking to hold his gaze. Too scared to keep up the pretense, she shifted her gaze to the floor and the black patent four-inch spike heels she had on. The skirts and blouses she wore every day might shout boring, but her shoes were 100-percent hooker.

She'd learned to wear clothes that didn't draw attention to her curves, only her cleavage, and she used her hair and shoes to further distract. Still, standing in front of Chase with the aid of extra height still left her feeling small. The top of her head might reach his chin. She'd guess he stood at least six feet three, if not taller. He simply dwarfed her. And for the first time in her life, she loved being short. It seemed to add to the sense of power he had over her.

"No." The blunt word shocked her. She stood speechless and rooted to her spot while he turned and walked back to his studio. No explanation, no further discussion, just no.

Just like that he'd found her not good enough? She fought the tears that threatened to fall as his abrupt rejection filtered through her thoughts. Eve looked at the front door and back at the studio Chase had disappeared into. She'd made the biggest fool of herself with no rock to crawl under. All of her fantasies about Chase came crashing down on her. Along with the hope she'd harbored that one day he would not only notice her, but desire her. All sucked dry by one tiny little word.

She wasn't good enough for Chase Miller. How could she have been so pathetic? The first tear splashed on her cheek and she ran for the exit.

.

TWO

Chase sat heavily in his desk chair and scrubbed his face with his hands. Dear God save him. The woman he'd allowed Murphy to hire for reception pushed every single button he possessed. From the first minute he'd laid eyes on her, he wanted her gone. So much so she'd become his obsession. A fact getting harder and harder to hide.

He thought of her day and night. Startling blue eyes that watched him with unadulterated lust every time he walked in the room. Gorgeous red hair down to her ass and what an ass it was. He itched to bend her over his bench and spank it until that perfect bottom was as red as her hair.

But it was her skin that mesmerized him. Pale and covered in freckles. Chase wanted to play connect the dots with his tongue and discover if every inch of her was covered by the sexy little spots. His imagination got the best of him when he thought endlessly of striping her ass and legs after he'd tied her up, of course.

There were various scenarios of predicament bondage he'd dreamed up for her. The kind of scene where the slightest movement became impossible and likely painful. The inner sadist in him smiled. She'd look sexy as hell tied in his ropes with Murphy on one side and him on the other. His cock twitched at the thought.

The photo shoot had obviously wound him up and Eve's offer was enough to make him forget her innocence. He'd spotted her submissive needs on day one, but no way in hell did she have the kind of knowledge and experience he needed in a girl. Oh but the temptation unnerved him. It wasn't as if he didn't have the patience to teach her. He could guide her through her submission and into the role as his personal submissive.

The door opened roughly and Murphy strode in. "What the hell happened with Eve?"

"What do you mean?"

"She just ran out of the office and I could have sworn I saw tears." He dropped onto the couch across the room and turned that suspicious gaze his way.

"I told you she was going to be trouble."

"That doesn't sound good," Murphy said.

He shook his head. "It's not. She volunteered for the latest Smith commission." Chase picked up the form he'd printed and handed it over to Murphy. A minute later a long, low whistle sounded from his friend.

"Damn. She'd be perfect."

"Yeah, exactly. Wait. What? Perfect. Are you crazy?" Chase leaned his chair to a near-reclining position and brushed the hair from his face. He was about three weeks past due for a haircut and it wouldn't stay out of his eyes. From there he rubbed his temples and hoped he could get the idea of Eve as his submissive out of his brain.

"Did she have any idea what she was asking for?"

"Probably not. She's asked a lot of questions since she arrived and we've both been completely honest with the extent of what we do here, but I doubt our little submissive wannabe has any real clue of what she'd be getting herself into."

"Not to mention you've got the worst hard-on for her."

Chase looked sharply at his friend. "Fuck you, man. I've seen you staring at her rack every chance you get. You're lucky she hasn't called sexual harassment on your ass."

"Me? Please. I'm not the one on the verge of biting her head off because you want in her pants so bad you can't think straight half the time." Murphy pulled himself from the couch and paced the length of the room. "I say we give her a chance. Show her the contract. If that doesn't scare her off, then maybe you're wrong about her."

"Easy for you to say. You just fucked your brains out."

"You know I can't resist a woman who begs. And she'd have been happy to service you as well. Jennifer is a sweet little professional subbie."

Chase tried to shake the images his camera captured today. A photographer was the ultimate voyeur and while he knew how to maintain control, this long dry spell he'd put himself through had begun to take its toll. It was time to head to Purgatory Club and begin a new search. Someone there would surely make him stop thinking about a certain bewitching little receptionist who dared him to take her with a guileless look.

"You can't resist any subbie. You're such a fucking horndog."

"Yeah, and since when is that a bad thing? You're either getting uptight in your old age or it's time for you to examine why this woman is under your skin."

"Old my ass." He didn't comment on the other half of his statement. Chase hated it when his friend was right. "Was she really crying when she left?" He loved to see a woman in tears, but not from his rejection. He'd rather see her writhing in his restraints, alternating between crying her eyes out and begging him to fuck her. His half-hard dick swelled more.

"Yeah, I was ready to run after her until you told me the deal. Since I'm not the one who rejected her, I think she needs to hear it from you."

Professionally he should stay the hell away from her. Personally he couldn't let her go. Not without talking to her.

With any luck, he'd explain what would be required of her and she'd run for the hills. There were reasons he didn't do hard-core shoots with amateurs. They were strenuous and fraught with high emotional impact. Not everyone could handle it.

"Chase, stop thinking about it and just talk to her. Not everything in this lifestyle has to fit your rigid standards. Sometimes you have to let nature take its course."

"Don't give me—"

"Just fucking talk to her."

* * *

Chase stared at the rundown apartment building in front of him and compared it to the address he'd hastily written on his notepad. The fact they matched stunned him. Why the hell did Eve live in a place like this? He pressed the lock button on his car remote and approached the building cautiously. The neighborhood didn't seem safe, much less the structure she lived in.

According to the address she provided she lived on the second floor. Chase opened the door and was immediately assaulted by a horrid smell. A mixture of pine cleaner and old. At least someone had given a halfhearted attempt to mask the fact this place threatened to crumble at any moment.

He gave a sideways glance to the elevator and decided against it. The stairs had to be a better choice. The open-to-the-outside stairwell did improve his opinion marginally as he took two steps at a time. In fact when he reached the landing he could have sworn he'd walked into a different building altogether. This floor looked at least like it had been renovated in this century. But the rest of the building...fuck.

Eve's door was the first on the right and he gave it a hard knock. He had half a mind to drag her out of here and find somewhere safe for her to live. Like his condo. The crazy thought formed before he had a chance to stop it. No way. Talk about your bad ideas with a capital Fucked-Up.

He heard noises from behind the door and waited as patiently as possible for her to open it.

"Chase, what do you want?" Her muffled question sounded through the door. *Guess the peephole works.*

"I'd like a few minutes of your time."

"No."

Her quick and abrupt answer brought a smile to his face. Turnabout was certainly fair play with this one. Okay, he'd play along for now. She deserved that much. "C'mon, Eve, give me a chance to explain. I am still your employer after all."

The only response he got was metal sliding on metal and a few seconds later she yanked the door open a few inches, a safety chain crossing in front of her face.

"I pretty much figured after I walked out today, my job would be gone. So that does not make you my boss and I do not have to talk to you."

She'd scrubbed her face clean of makeup and she wore a simple thin-strap tank top and yoga-style pants that gently hugged the gorgeous curves of her hips and legs. Without those insanely sexy shoes she wore every day he noticed how short she really was. With her petite stature and no make up she looked young. But instead of looking like a child, her clean face and simple clothes gave him a sense of sweet vulnerability. Now he wished he'd brought his camera.

"Is that what you want? To quit?" Chase shouldered the door and moved closer. "Let me come in for a few minutes so we can talk about it." If she really wanted to leave, then he finally had his way out of the torture he'd suffered. He could simply walk away now and be done with the whole mess. He'd go to the club tonight and find a willing play partner and go from there.

You don't want her to go. Murphy's mocking statement haunted him.

She looked unsure. The slight narrowing of her eyes and the tiny purse of her mouth gave her thoughts away. Patience. He normally had it in spades and he could employ it here. Let her make the decisions *for now*. Come to him. It couldn't be any other way. For the shoot or anything else he had to ensure her trust. Nothing was more important.

After a few minutes of their showdown, she relented, closing the door and unfastening her security chain. Chase never understood why people put any faith into those silly lightweight mechanisms. It took nothing to push the door and make it break. A woman living alone in a neighborhood like this needed far better security. This may not be New York City but that didn't mean women weren't attacked or worse. He added that to his running mental list of things he needed to get done. A new source of security for his receptionist.

When she opened the door she stood back and motioned with her hand for him to enter. He bit back the satisfied smile as he envisioned this the first win in the many battles of will to come. Murphy was right. He wasn't about to let her go.

Stepping into her modest-sized apartment was like walking into a different building. She'd gone to great lengths to mask the rundown place she lived in by decorating her private space in a sort of shabby Old World style. The cracks in the walls gave the purple and gold paint treatment character. The vibrant space with pillows everywhere, furniture restyled from cast-offs and more color than the average color wheel could only be described as eye-popping.

Who the hell was this woman? For the first time since he'd met her, he looked beyond the beauty and luscious curves to realize he knew next to nothing about her.

"Wow, this is quite a transformation from the rest of your building." He walked the perimeter of the area, peering into the few doors that led off the main room. Color and style met him everywhere.

"It's amazing what you can do with a little imagination and a can of paint or two." She spoke quietly from near the door as if afraid to come too close to him.

"You have the eye of an artist. What are you doing working as my receptionist with talent like this?"

"It's no big deal. Besides, I don't have a lot of experience. Do you know how few people in this town are willing to take a chance on someone without it?" She edged to the couch and took a seat in one corner, immediately covering most of her body by hugging a fat purple pillow to her chest.

"Are you afraid of me, Eve?" He didn't like the wary look on her face. She seemed skittish.

"I don't know how to be with you after this afternoon," she whispered.

Chase winced at the obvious damage his gruff behavior had caused. *Way to go, dumbass.*

"I didn't mean for you to take it personally. The requirements attached to that commission are pretty intense. Not something I would normally consider an amateur for."

She turned away from him, but not before he noticed the lovely shade of crimson blooming across her face.

"I wouldn't have volunteered if I didn't have an idea of what I was getting into. I'm not stupid."

Her insolence gave him dirtier thoughts than it should. He needed to get out of here before he did something stupid, like fuck her. His hard-on grew along with the increasing images that filtered through his mind. The couch she sat on had been created from an old wrought-iron bed frame with knobs and spindles, perfect to tie her to. Hell, the entire apartment was a rigger's dream. The open ceiling beams alone gave him a myriad of ideas for photographs. He could already imagine her in an old-fashioned corset and leggings with her hair piled on top of her head.

Her body shape would make a delicious pinup shoot.

Bettie Page had nothing on her, and a bondage artist like Murphy would think he'd died and gone to heaven in a place like this. Chase made another mental note to bring his camera the next time he visited.

First things first. "I never thought you were stupid. But there are things in the order that could send you or anyone not accustomed to them, running for the hills and well, Murphy kind of likes having you around as the receptionist."

"Murphy likes having me around." Not a question, but a statement that implied the question. Despite the urges this woman created, he'd come here to offer her a job and in doing so had to remain professional. So he ignored that statement instead of showing her what he thought of having her around. He reached into his jacket and pulled a small manila folder from the pocket. He laid the folder on the coffee table and pushed it in her direction.

"The rejection really wasn't personal. Appearance-wise we couldn't ask for a more perfect model." He enjoyed watching her eyes widen in surprise and her mouth open to say something and then close again when she changed her mind. He could practically see the gears turning in her head as she tried to figure him out.

Little did she know he thrived on keeping a submissive off balance.

"I'm not convinced you truly understand what you offered yourself up for, but I've decided to let you read for yourself and then decide." He held up his hand to stop her response. "No, until you read through this you're not ready. Even then you may not be. So I've outlined the exact client requirements for you and included a copy of the hard-core model contract. If, and only if, you read it thoroughly and answer all the questions in it can you give me an answer. Do you understand?"

"Yes, sir." Her simple answer made his dick swell more. It didn't matter that her use of *Sir* probably only came out of respect for an employer, not a Dom. The sound uttered from her lips enflamed a need that had been sizzling for weeks and it was about to burn out of control.

"Tell me about your bondage experience. Have you even been restrained before?" Again she blushed to the roots of her hair, and he sighed in resignation. A complete novice would never work. He should snatch the folder and hightail it out of here. Until he noticed the sheen of tears swimming in her eyes.

"Once," she uttered.

Chase sighed. She wasn't going to make this easy for him, and the thought of having to drag it out of her did not sound fun. "And?"

"And I don't want to talk about it." She tossed the pillow aside and pulled her legs underneath her chin.

Alarm bells went off for Chase. Time to say forget it and get the hell out of Dodge. "Just tell me one thing and I'll let it go for now. Did someone hurt you?"

The air in the room grew thick and heavy in the few seconds she didn't answer. She pulled her bottom lip between her teeth and shook her head. A huge sigh of relief swept through Chase. Unfortunately stories of women being taken too far or being used badly in the name of BDSM were all too frequent in the community, and the thought of someone taking advantage of this one twisted his gut.

"I'm not looking to be rescued, Chase. I'm a big girl capable of making my own decisions. Despite my earlier behavior, I do know how to keep my emotions in check. I've paid attention to what goes on around the studio and I've studied many of your photos. But I haven't been with a man in over two years, and I need this. It's time for me to stop wishing and start doing. Please, give me a chance."

Chase sat stunned at her revelation. Now he definitely wanted to know more. He had so many questions he didn't know where to start.

She picked up the folder. "Do you want me to read this now? Are you going to insist on watching me go through every word?"

Ooh, the sass. He had just the thing for a mouth like that. Unfortunately he couldn't go there — yet. "No." He stood and moved toward the door. "You read through it and decide by morning. Either way, you still have a job at Altered Ego and I'll expect you at the office at nine a.m. sharp with your cute shoes and a decision."

Eve had stood from the couch and walked in the direction of the front door while he spoke, and now he took two strides toward her. She stepped back. "If you sign that contract, there will be no going back. Everything changes, no matter how hard you try."

THREE

Eve leaned against the door and breathed deep. Chase's sensual threat had gone straight to her sex despite her best intentions. Hell, everything about the damned man went straight there. He personified hot sex with his gorgeous looks, but his voice was pure sin. She'd been horrified to find him at her door. Ever since she'd fled from the office today, she'd heard nothing but "no" over and over in her head. And the look on his face when he'd uttered it tortured her.

Now he'd come and gone, not with an apology but with an excuse for why he'd reacted the way he had. And a folder. She'd read his damned contract, but she didn't care what the hell it said.

After two years of nothing but sickness and death, with no man in sight, she needed a boost when it came to getting her life back on track. This—she opened the folder and stared at the requirements — this would teach her once and for all if the fantasies she harbored could be more than mere figments of her imagination. Being submissive for Chase's camera would give her a taste of what the real thing could be.

It was no accident she'd been drawn to Altered Ego when a position opened up. Fate had shone down on her. If Chase had gone a step closer to her bedroom, he would have seen a very familiar sight. Eve had ordered more than one of his black-and-white erotic prints from his Web site and had them framed and hung in her bedroom.

When she'd decided to gut her father's apartment and start from scratch, she'd saved her bedroom for last. Chase and Murphy inspired quite a bit of the design without even knowing it. Eve wandered into her room and curled up on the big, plush bed. She glanced at the half-empty bottle of wine she'd been working her way through before she'd been interrupted. There'd be more of that later.

Exhaling a shaky breath, she laid out the folder in front of her and opened the flap. The familiar logo of Altered Ego was emblazoned across the top of the paper with the details listed below.

Her gaze skimmed to the pertinent information she sought. Words such as "insertion," "predicament," and "forced orgasms" leaped from the page. Panic swelled inside her, alongside the familiar sensation of fear. She tamped down those feelings and straightened her spine. *They are just words typed out on white paper. Nothing to be afraid of.*

She forced herself to breathe deep and exhale slowly and start at the beginning. This client wanted a long list of things to be included in the commission. Some would require clothes and some would not. All of them included her being restrained in some fashion, with an emphasis on rope bondage instead of cuffs or shackles.

The sessions would be long in order for Chase and Murphy to create the artistry the client requested, and her job would be to do more than simply lie there and go along for the ride. There were a myriad of emotions marked on the standard checklist. Eve turned the page, unwilling to linger on the details for too long. She wouldn't be deterred.

The standard contract had far more detail, but Chase didn't know she'd already seen one of these. One of the models had dropped one off last week, and since the envelope had not been sealed, curiosity got the better of her. Pretty much by signing this document, she gave permission to Altered Ego, and Chase and Murphy by way of ownership, to do anything they saw fit during a shoot.

Including sex for photographic purposes.

Nerves fluttered in her stomach at the thought of being taken by Murphy while Chase captured the pictures. A quick twinge of guilt caught her off guard, which she quickly pushed away. Good girls weren't supposed to be this excited about the cold, clinical way these acts were portrayed in black and white. This wasn't a date, nor was it a romance, she reminded herself. She had something to prove to herself, and she wanted to do something different. Something so far outside her comfort zone she'd never want to go back. She didn't want to be the good girl anymore. It was time to be the bad girl.

She hastily picked up a pen she'd left lying on the nightstand, and signed across the dotted line.

Fuck it.

If she couldn't take a chance with someone like Chase, she never would. He'd maintained a strange distance between them most of the time, yet she still got to know him a little. She trusted him not to hurt her. At least physically. If they did half of what was listed in that contract it wouldn't be easy to stay detached. One orgasm could lead to another and then what? Chase and Murphy liked to work together and they made a great team. If she got attached there would be trouble.

Eve sat up straighter and grabbed her glass of wine. Bad girls didn't fall in love every time a man had sex with her. That was the point of being a bad girl, right? She could do this. Her plan was to go in and keep her heart guarded at all times. Together they would do a job and she'd maybe learn if the lifestyle was indeed something she wanted to pursue like she thought.

In the end she would walk away with some new experience and no regret.

Right?

* * *

Precisely at nine a.m. sharp, Eve swiped her employee card through the security pad on the back door of the industrial building that housed the photo studio. Both Chase's and Murphy's cars were already in the parking lot. She'd carefully chosen one of the most conservative business suits she owned, along with the most outrageous pair of five-inch heels she possessed. They were black with hot pink straps that buckled across the top of her foot and around her ankle. They'd reminded her of a bondage photo she'd seen in Chase's office and until now she'd not had the nerve to wear them

Underneath the conservative part of outfit was also a completely different story. After the first few weeks of working at Altered Ego, she'd begun to change how she dressed underneath her plain skirts and blouses. She'd been determined to feel sexy despite her size and ordered all new lingerie. On days she felt particularly scandalous, she would wear no panties underneath her skirt and a thin lace bra that did little to hide her hard nipples poking underneath.

Today was not one of those days.

She'd picked matching black lace panties and bra. Chase had given her no indication of when the shoot would begin if she accepted, so she'd decided to come prepared just in case. At the front entrance, she grasped the handle on the frosted glass door and pulled it open. Eve half expected Chase and Murphy to be standing in the lobby waiting for her. Instead the hum of the aquarium in the corner greeted her along with the scent of freshly brewed coffee.

Mmm. A super shot of caffeine sounded like the perfect way to start her day. No messages sat on her desk, and everything remained exactly as she'd left it the afternoon before. Eve dropped her bag and the folder on her desk and headed in the direction of the small kitchen. She hadn't gotten three feet away when the intercom buzzed.

"Eve, did you bring the Smith folder with you this morning?" The tone of Chase's question told her nothing. She wasn't surprised. He probably excelled at card games with that damned poker face of his.

She rushed as fast as she could on five-inch heels back to her desk, depressed the intercom button, and spoke. "Yes, sir, it's here on my desk."

"Could you please bring it in?"

"Of course." *Oh boy, here we go.* He hadn't even let her get her morning coffee before she had to face him with her answer. Eve scooped up the folder and headed for Chase's office. No doubt he and Murphy would be waiting and Chase would have told him everything about their conversation from the night before.

Outside his door, she plastered on her hopeful smile and entered his space. Chase didn't look up from his computer, nor did he greet her in any way. She waited a few seconds, unsure how to proceed.

"I've got the file here for you. I —"

"Good." He interrupted. "Just leave it there in my box."

Shocked by his apparent disinterest, Eve dropped the file, turned, and walked out the door. After everything she'd put herself through in anticipation of seeing him this morning, the letdown of being summarily dismissed crippled her.

Back at her desk with coffee forgotten, she fell into her chair and stared at her computer screen. Why hadn't he said anything? He didn't even ask if she'd signed the agreement. And where the hell was Murphy? She'd already noticed that his office was empty this morning and had assumed he'd be waiting with Chase. She poked her head over the partition and stared in the direction of the studio. Sure enough the door was closed tight and the busy light was on. She leafed through the appointment book to see what was scheduled, only to find they had nothing until eleven o'clock this morning.

So why then was Murphy shut in the studio and Chase sitting in his office staring at the screen? She had half a mind to head into the dressing room and take a peek, but the chance of getting caught was too great. Certainly her boss would not be pleased if he discovered her spying on a session.

Hours passed as Eve went about her morning routine. Answering calls and sorting through e-mails as well as what was delivered by the mailman. Every time Eve moved, the lace of her bra rubbed across her nipples until they'd gone beyond sensitive to wildly aroused. Constant images of Chase and Murphy surrounding her flooded her mind. Simply every move, every thought kept her continuously on edge until she thought she'd go mad.

She'd glance at the clock and squirm endlessly in her chair, the wait excruciating. She'd expected Chase to give her a hard time this morning, to try and talk her out of the job. Them ignoring her had never crossed her mind. It served as a stark reminder that this was simply a job. Not a date. Not a love affair. A job that she'd signed a contract to do.

Still, her panties stayed wet and her budded tips brushing against fabric made it difficult for her not to moan. Not exactly the kind of professional behavior they probably expected. Sweat dotted her forehead as she crossed and uncrossed her legs.

Fuck.

If it wasn't her nipples, it was her clit. Eve inhaled a slow, steady breath and sat completely still. If she could slow her pulse, she could certainly get things back under control. This kind of wanton behavior was not her. She picked up the bottle of water on her desk and with shaky hands brought it to her lips. Cool water splashed down her throat. She wished she could dump it over her head. Maybe then she'd stop thinking about being touched. Or imagining what Chase looked like underneath his clothing.

Not once in all of her spying had he so much as removed a shirt. Of course that didn't stop her from noticing the way the muscles moved and bunched the cloth as he worked, though. Or the way the muscles in his forearm flexed as he moved. God, what the hell was wrong with her?

Eve gave up trying to slow her breathing and gulped for much-needed air instead. Perspiration trailed down her spine and into the edge of her skirt. If they didn't say something soon, she'd have to go to the restroom and get herself off. Whatever it took to take the edge off. Why wait?

So far nothing had happened and she owed them nothing. Chase and his fucking computer could take a flying leap for keeping her at bay like this. Making her wonder what he planned to do as if this were just any old ordinary day and not the one where she'd made an epic decision to change her life.

She smoothed down the edge of her skirt and straightened her spine. Five minutes in the bathroom was all she needed. Maybe less. Screw Chase and the horse he rode in on. She didn't need this bullshit. She fucking needed relief. A few seconds later, only three feet lay between her and relief as she headed for the restroom.

"Come into the studio," Chase commanded from the doorway closest to her.

Her heart lurched in her chest, a gasp falling from her mouth. "Jesus, Chase, you scared the hell out of me."

He quirked his brows in her direction before turning away to stride back into the studio he'd mysteriously come from. Hours and hours she'd waited, and she'd never noticed he came out of his office and went into the studio. What else didn't she notice?

She needed to wash her face and freshen up. The way she'd been stressing the last hour had to show in her appearance by now. With a last wistful glance at the bathroom, she hurried through the door to the studio. Some trouble just wasn't worth it, and if they wanted to talk to her about the modeling job, she'd best not keep them waiting. Besides, she got the distinct impression that Chase expected to be obeyed.

Feeling hot and surly, she barely refrained from sticking her tongue out at his back. Her nerves from the morning had finally quieted down, and her interest in all of this had waned. She spotted Murphy splayed out on the velvet couch in the corner with various props spread on the seat next to him. Coils of black rope, a red flogger, and a short brown leather riding crop.

Instantly her panties dampened and her heart raced. So much for playing it cool.

"Stand there." Chase pointed to the middle of the room. Where a spotlight shone bright. Eve complied, silently moving except for the click of her heels on the wood floor. Whatever happened next, she desperately hoped she could go through with it. Because standing still, knowing that Murphy watched her every move, unnerved her more than she'd expected.

Chase picked up one of his cameras and turned to face her. He looked her over from head to toe before examining her through the lens. Each click of the camera shutter thundered through the room, nearly matching the roughshod beat of her racing pulse.

"Since you brought in a signed contract, I'm not going to ask again if you're sure. You'll simply follow the instructions either of us give." Chase didn't let up with the pictures, and other than stand there and wait, she didn't know what else to do.

"Relax. Don't tense up. No one is going to hurt you. *Much.*"

Murphy snickered from the couch behind her at Chase's last comment. She thought she knew exactly how things would go, but now she wasn't so sure.

"Lose the skirt and blouse."

Compelled to move, Eve reached behind her and grasped the hook at the waistband of her skirt. Her hands trembled. This wasn't at all the picture she'd imagined in her head.

"Allow me." Murphy breathed into her ear. He'd silently moved from the couch and now brushed her hand aside. Deft fingers finessed the hook open and slid the zipper down. Warm hands caressed her bare waist, sweeping the fabric down her hips and thighs. Suddenly, cool air rushed across her lace-covered sex, causing Eve to gasp at the sudden sensation.

Murphy kept silent while he worked, although this close he had to know exactly how aroused she was. She stepped gingerly from her skirt so as not to lose her balance. Even with practice, these heels were treacherous.

Automatically her hands went to the tiny buttons of her blouse.

Murphy grabbed her wrist and stopped her. "I will do it." The hardened tone of his voice sent shivers racing up and down her spine. He cupped her chin and brought her gaze to his. "Eyes on me, sexy."

Oh Lord, he was beautiful.

With eyes the color of deep dark chocolate staring into her, it was all Eve could do not to moan in ecstasy. The heated look he gave her melted her insides as he unhooked one button at a time until her shirt lay open, his fingers brushing the roundness of her stomach. Nervous currents of electricity zapped through her with every new touch. She desperately wanted to squeeze her eyes shut and hide from the momentary embarrassment of the most gorgeous man she'd ever laid eyes on touching her. *Her.*

Murphy stepped close to push the offending shirt from her shoulders. Heat enveloped her, warmed her through. It took every ounce of willpower not to reach for him, to pull him close and rub all over him. He smelled so fucking good. A little like sex and a lot like wild man. Maybe it was the persona she'd built around him. But as far as she could tell, he lived up to every bad boy, sex-starved fantasy she'd included him in.

Suddenly, the heat was gone and Murphy stood back so Chase could take more pictures. The camera clicked continuously, and she swore he had to have photographed every blessed inch of her body when he finally stopped and brought the camera to his side.

"Why are you here, Eve?"

"To prove to myself that even curves are erotic," she blurted out without thinking.

Chase's eyes narrowed. "Bullshit."

Eve blinked. Shocked by the harsh word. "It's true." She dug her teeth into her bottom lip for a second, waiting for him to say something else. Instead they both stared her down, and she had a sudden need to crawl out of her own skin. "What? What more do you want from me?"

A rough laugh rumbled from Chase, and Murphy turned away. "I want you to tell me everything. The camera doesn't lie and by the time we're through I will know all of your secrets. Are you ready for that?"

She nodded. Half sick with worry.

"What's your biggest fantasy?"

Eve sighed. That was easy. "To be tied up and ravished." She had to look away.

"But it's not that simple, is it?" Chase obviously wasn't going to back down. Figuring out what to say while standing half-naked under white hot lights with two men staring intently at her wasn't easy.

"Let's try another question." Chase lifted the camera to his face and took another series of photos. "Why haven't you been fucked in two years?"

Murphy's head swung in Chase's direction. "What?"

"That's what she told me, and I want to know why. If something happened that caused her to withdraw, I don't want to find out in the middle of a session. I won't be responsible for traumatizing her further."

"It's not like that at all." Anger surged through her. "I meant what I said last night. No one ever hurt me." Fuck, she'd obviously made a mistake. Eve reached down for her clothes.

"Don't." The command from Chase boomed around her, and she paused with her hand halfway to the floor. She peeked at his face, and the dark warning in his eyes told her to listen. To take a step back and not be rash. Slowly, she stood, but now doubts nagged at her mind.

Murphy stepped forward and smiled sweetly at her. "Don't let the big bad Chase freak you out. You have to understand there isn't anything more irresponsible than scening with someone you aren't sure about. Just because you've agreed to model doesn't absolve us of your well-being. In fact, it makes the trust between us more important than ever. Fetish models work hard and it's our duty to make sure they get what they need."

Murphy moved behind her and caressed her arms with a featherlight brush. She found his touch so mesmerizing, she almost didn't notice Chase had resumed taking pictures. It was nearly impossible to think beyond the warm caresses and whispered reassurances he plied her with.

"Tell me. Since I wasn't there when you and Chase discussed this I need to know. Why would such a remarkable woman go untouched for so long? It's almost criminal."

Eve shivered, long tremors raced down her spine. "It's not at all what you think."

"And how do you know what I think?" he whispered at her ear.

"Because the truth is sad and has nothing to do with this." Her legs trembled, and her stomach pitched to think of everything she'd been through these last two years. She'd basically been reduced to a 24-7 nurse with nothing but responsibilities.

Murphy pulled back, the sexiness wiped from his face and replaced with concern. "It sounds important enough for us to know, but I'll let it go for now. But, Eve" — he cupped her chin — "no one can ever really be what you need until you're willing to tell them everything. *Everything*."

Relief sagged through her. Going through this was hard enough without thinking of the grief that had ripped her life in two. Still, watching Murphy's back as he retreated from her created a longing that surprised her. Just once in her life she needed… "I need to experience a man stronger than myself," she blurted. Anything to keep this from ending here.

FOUR

Chase lowered his camera, and Murphy froze next to him.

"What did you say?" Surprised and intrigued by her outburst, he set down his camera on the small worktable stationed next to the floodlight. Suddenly the need to touch her overwhelmed him as he watched her stand up straight and raise her chin with a newfound courage.

"Please, for once let me feel what it's like to not have to be in control. To not have to stress over every detail. To be someone else, even if it's just one day. Please, Chase, I need this."

He ignored the barely there moan that sounded from Murphy to study the woman in front of him. Her eyes shone with unshed tears that clearly took everything she had to contain. Apparently their receptionist had more layers than even he'd thought. However, without full knowledge there were a variety of things that could go wrong. Her inability to share the trauma that disrupted her life should have had him escorting her out of his studio. Yet, he knew he wouldn't.

Without turning from Eve, Chase spoke to Murphy. "Get the chair."

"As for you." He lowered his voice and moved close. "I hope you understand what you're asking for. This goes beyond a few pictures." He curved around her side and stood behind her. He was close enough to feel her body heat without touching her. The contrast of the black lace of her undergarments against her creamy flesh pleased the eye of the photographer, but the man wanted to rip the offending coverings away so he'd have an unobstructed view of what he wanted.

He opted for a compromise since they had plenty of time to explore. "The camera will show me, and I have no problem taking you as far as I need to in order to expose the woman underneath. But first, tell me you want this." Chase unclasped the hooks that held her bra in place, pushed the straps from her shoulder and allowed it to drop to the floor. The sexy hitch in her breathing pleased him immensely, even more so when she didn't object. Pale, freckled skin beckoned him. Her ample breasts would more than fill his hands, but it was the taut, jutting nipples that informed him how much more she needed.

"I want this."

Without the camera acting as a barrier between them, he couldn't resist touching her. His hands spanned a good portion of her waist—soft, delicate skin he longed to see abraded by rope. Rich amber hair floated down her back with a scent of lavender and some spice he couldn't name. But the color drew him like a living, breathing flame. Every sexual thought he'd had since she'd arrived had something to do with the hue of her hair.

Sinful, decadent thoughts that always led to her begging for more while he captured every expression on film. Reluctantly, he withdrew when Murphy arrived with the black oak chair and rope he'd already laid out. A gentle push on her shoulder was all it took for her to bend her knees and take a cautious seat.

"Sit back and try to relax. You're going to be in this position for a while." Chase let Murphy get to work while he retrieved some new lenses. As much as he wanted to photograph her, he also wanted to fuck her. Or better yet, photograph her while she sucked him off. His cock twitched in his pants on that one. Yeah, he hoped the little minx had it in her, because he planned to stress some of her limits before the day was over.

"Ready," Murphy called from behind him.

Chase turned and nearly swallowed his tongue at the sight in front of him. Murphy and his Cheshire-smug grin stared back at him.

"Pretty, isn't she?"

"'Pretty' doesn't do her justice." Murphy had banded her to the back of the chair from shoulder to hip with the rope crossing horizontally across her body, both above and below her breasts. Her legs splayed open with only a scrap of lace covering what Chase instinctively knew would be heaven on earth. It took every ounce of restraint not to rip the fabric from her and reveal the pussy he ached for.

Her arms were bound behind the chair as well, and Murphy had gotten creative and added a black silk blindfold. An excellent implement that gave Chase some ideas for how the day would end. He brought the digital camera to his face, being sure to perfect the focus. Although he planned every kind of shot possible today.

"Are you comfortable, Eve?" Chase asked the question while zooming in for a close-up on her mouth. The red gloss she'd covered her lips with struck him with temptation as if she were a matador with a red flag and he'd become the charging bull.

She nodded, and Murphy must have read his mind. His finger tapped her lips and instructed her to remain silent. She wouldn't be permitted to see what was going on around her or speak unless there was an emergency. Deep down, Chase knew Murphy had the heart of a sadist and would one day require a submissive to become his slave.

Minutes stretched into hours while Chase examined every inch of Eve through his lens. By the time they finished this commission, he'd know the canvas of her body better than she did. Now that he'd gotten the basic photographs he wanted from her today, it was time to step things up.

"Grab her hair," Chase demanded.

Murphy perked up from his seat on the couch and grinned. "All right, party time." He swiped the black T-shirt he wore over his head and tossed it on the seat. Bare chest, leather pants, and combat-style boots were the perfect look for what Chase had in mind.

The subtle shift in Eve's mouth and limbs indicated she'd heard their words and was fully alert.

Good.

Murphy clutched a handful of red silk and tugged her head back, baring her throat. For now Murphy knew exactly what to do, and Chase settled back in for the shots. Time for her to be ravished, as she'd so delicately put it earlier. Although what Murphy was about to do to her in no way resembled anything delicate.

Murphy's head dipped to the delicious column of her neck, and Chase took up a side angle position to capture her reactions. Murphy nipped at her throat, and a whimper sounded from Eve. Tongue, teeth, and lips devoured her flesh until her breath came in gasping pants. Even

Murphy seemed to have forgotten the camera as he followed the trail down to the tight rosy nipples that practically begged to be touched. Or better yet, clamped.

The zipper of Chase's jeans dug into the skin of his dick as he grew fucking hard as steel. The job was often a turn-on, but this was ridiculous. His balls swelled and hung heavy between his legs until the photographs were no longer the priority. Every time Murphy bit particularly hard on one of her nipples, she jerked the chair, and his cock moved right along with it.

The marks Murphy left on her skin would photograph beautifully, and Chase knew his client would be immensely pleased. For a second, a vicious moment of protectiveness reared its ugly head inside him. If he claimed her, like he continued to consider, handing over pictures of her would fucking piss him off.

"Are you wet yet, baby?" Murphy's question pulled Chase from his ugly thoughts, and his gaze flew to her pussy. The panties wouldn't last much longer.

"Yes," she whispered.

"Ah ah ah. No talking, remember? I ask simple questions that require no more than a movement of your head. For that you've earned your first punishment." Murphy gave her no time to protest or ponder before he grabbed a nipple and twisted hard.

On the inevitable gasp that tore from Eve, Murphy released the precious bud. A smile quirked at his lips. They definitely had her attention now. The pain at her nipple had instinctively caused her to cant her hips in Murphy's direction, a movement he might have missed without his camera.

Not being able to see what was coming not only kept her on the edge, it allowed her the freedom to explore something her mind might object to if she knew about it in advance. It was definitely a psychological game, and one his little Eve desperately needed in order to work through some of her barriers.

Murphy went back to his exploration as he caressed every spot of bare flesh available. When his hands were on her thighs and his thumbs perilously close to the edge of her panties, the camera caught the trembling of her bottom lip. God, her pictures would be exquisite.

"Do you know how much I've fantasized about this, Eve?" Murphy spoke quietly.

Her teeth dug into her bottom lip, and she shook her head.

"I've thought about this incredible body a lot. How perfect these curves are for my ropes." His finger disappeared underneath the black lace, and Chase nearly choked with the need to find out for himself what she felt like. He reached for his dick and pushed down on it, hoping against hope for some relief.

"Oh hell. Hot, slick, and even wetter than I expected." Murphy crooned while he fucked his finger in and out of her sweet, sweet pussy. "Do you want me to stop, sugar?"

Her head moved from side to side in fast, jerky movements. She opened her mouth to speak and slammed it shut at the last minute. Probably remembering she'd been forbidden to speak.

Enjoy that control for now, sweet Eve. Before long you'll forget all about it and be begging for release.

FIVE

Eve's eyes rolled to the back of her head at the pleasure storming through her. Murphy's wicked manipulation of her aching sex drove her fast and hard to the edge of what promised to be an out of this world explosion.

She tried to buck her hips to increase the friction, but the ropes she'd momentarily forgotten about restricted her movement. Her pleasure was at the complete mercy of Murphy's whim. Frustration at his maddeningly slow pace erupted in the form of a series of whimpers.

"I think she likes it." Murphy's voice mocked her predicament, and the deep hum of agreement from Chase inflamed everything swirling inside her. Damn them for this. If he'd just angle his finger a little higher and rub her...

"Enough." The harsh command from Chase startled her. But the withdrawal of Murphy's touch left her breathless and hot. She couldn't take this teasing any longer. Not after sitting tied for so long with nothing to do but think about everything she couldn't see. The sound of Chase taking hundreds of pictures, Murphy stirring on the couch, and occasionally someone breathing heavily. Her arms ached, but she'd passed pain and fear a while ago and was left with a constant ache she found oddly comforting. Which of course made no sense at all.

Until Murphy had touched her. In an instant she'd gone up in flames, and the need for their touch became more painful than anything she'd experienced thus far.

"Please," she whispered, breaking the rules. It didn't matter. In fact nothing at all mattered other than the two men she knew stood just in front of her. Waiting for what, she had no idea.

"Please what?" Chase's voice sounded next to her ear. So close his breath caressed her face. Tears sprang to her eyes. He was right here. So close she could smell him. Warm skin with the faintest tang of sweat. Her mouth watered at the thought of tasting him, of licking the side of his neck from shoulder to ear.

"Need — touch." Even the harsh crack of her voice didn't faze her. "Please."

"I could fuck you now, Eve, couldn't I?"

"Yes," she answered with a heavy breath. "Yes — that — now." He could do anything he wanted as long as he didn't stop touching her.

"Would you give me anything I wanted? No matter what it was?"

Chase's question straight from her head caught her off guard. Her mind warred between answering yes and thinking logically. What if he made her do something truly awful? A fresh stab of fear pierced through the lust swamping her.

"That's what I thought. You aren't yet ready to fully submit. Let's try something else." Displaced air brushed her face as she imagined Chase moving away from her. Oh God, no, he couldn't walk away now.

"I'm sorry—I don't know—" The stark sound of metal scraping against metal when a zipper was released distracted her from her thoughts. Maybe he'd decided to do it anyway.

"Open your mouth, baby, and suck me."

For a split second, Eve's mind reeled. She squeezed her eyes tight behind the blindfold and instinctively obeyed. Smooth, searing-hot flesh slid between her lips, the fat crown of Chase's cock brushing against her tongue. She moaned at the overwhelming sensation and taste of this man. He felt like solid steel encased in velvet-soft skin stretched taut. She'd done this to him...

The thought that he ached as much as she did for this undid her.

Eve stretched her mouth wider, wanting more of him, wanting every inch she could possibly take. He fed her several more inches before pulling back out, leaving only the tip to rest on her tongue. Liquid heat spread from her tingling scalp to the tips of her toes, tightening her nipples to near pain and flooding her sex with so much moisture she ached with need. Never in her life had her cravings become so intense so fast.

She screamed in her head for him to please keep going, but the helplessness of her situation gave her absolutely no control. She moaned around his thick cock instead, her tongue vibrating against him. His resulting groan encouraged her to work harder. Eve tightened her lips around his shaft and sucked as hard as she could.

"Ahhhhh."

His moans encouraged her to keep going. To do everything possible to please him until he too lost a little bit of his legendary control.

"Harder." She didn't recognize the hard, guttural voice demanding more from her. Eve's pussy responded to his need with a rush of blood to her groin. Her clit swelled, and she seriously began to think she'd go insane if someone didn't touch her.

More of his hard length slipped between her lips, and Eve swallowed him until he hit the back of her throat. She struggled against the bindings on her arms at the thought of digging her fingers into his thighs and gaining leverage for her movements. Tears of frustration sprang to her eyes over what little she could do. If her hands were free, she'd be able to cup his balls and squeeze the sensitive sac, giving him even more pleasure.

Moving her head, she slid up and down his shaft, her tongue flicking continuously along the underside. In between each new thrust she took a few seconds to suck hard on the pulsing crown, pulling moans from him each time. Pleasure continued to rise in her body as he grew harder, his movements getting choppy.

His fingers dug into her hair, giving him the leverage for his insistent strokes. She had him now. Her helplessness transformed into power, the kind that suddenly freed her to take more of what Chase wanted to give. Somehow she relaxed her throat and he slipped farther inside. Free to accept his possession, her sex throbbed mercilessly while the rest of her trembled in desperate rhythm with his hips. Blood roared in her ears until the groans and words from Chase became indiscernible.

One hand moved down to grab on to her shoulder, his fingers tightening on her skin. His dick swelled, stretching her jaw to its limit.

A loud cry broke through the fog in her head at the same time heated jets of his release spurted to the back of her throat. With the salty essence exploding on her tongue, the blindfold was yanked from her eyes. Even in the dim light, she squinted against the shock of sudden brightness.

"Fuck yeah, baby, swallow it all."

Her lids lifted, and she nearly choked in surprise. It wasn't Chase fucking her mouth. No, the cum she so greedily took came from Murphy.

Moments later he released her head and shoulder and brushed her cheek. His cock slipped from her lips, and she inhaled sharply. God, she didn't know what to think anymore. He'd tricked her. She'd thought of Chase the entire time the cock was in her mouth. Although she had no regrets that it had been Murphy. Her body buzzed with need and here, like this, she couldn't deny she'd wanted both of them. Still did. Heat flooded her cheeks at the self-confession.

Eve tried to steady her breathing, but it was impossible with the wall of pleasure pressing down on her. She glanced around the room and searched for Chase with no success.

"He isn't here anymore," Murphy stated. He pushed his cock back into his leathers and refastened them. The lingering sensation of him urgently taking her mouth filled her mind. The hum of arousal inside her had moved to a full roar, and Murphy made no move to touch her. In fact, the look on his face seemed that of regret.

Eve wanted to say something, to beg him to help her, but she couldn't do it. The moment she'd been hoping for had passed with Chase's exit.

Whenever the hell that had happened. Now her body buzzed with an energy that had nowhere to go. Bitter resentment filled her despite the pleasure she'd experienced only moments ago. Even knowing it was partially Murphy's command she'd been under couldn't take that away from her. She'd loved having his cock in her mouth and relished the thought of doing it again and again.

Still. Her inability to hold Chase's focus pained her. Why didn't he want her too? Her brain worked frantically to figure it out while panic rose at her inability to move. Eve thrashed in the chair, pulling at her restraints.

"Eve, stop." Murphy cupped her cheeks and forced her gaze to his. "Relax. Everything is fine, baby. You did such an amazing job today. I know Chase is extremely pleased with what he saw."

"I don't care about the pictures. It wasn't the point," she said. A heavy pit had settled in her stomach, and she needed to get out of here. Her mind was on overload and she couldn't take it anymore. "Untie me."

Murphy didn't hesitate. He moved behind her and went to work on her restraints. The more he tugged on the rope, the harder she fought back, trying to free herself. Her arms tingled, and she wasn't sure she could feel her hands.

"Stop. Calm down. You're making it harder for me to get you undone. Stop struggling and give me a few minutes to get you free."

Eve stilled at the firm tone of his voice. Her heart beat frantically, but she worked to settle herself down. *Don't panic. Don't panic. Don't panic.*

"You're loose now, but I need you to remain calm. Let me take care of you." Murphy lifted her from the chair and carried her to the couch. He sank into the leather and settled her on top of him with her back facing his front. He gently began massaging her right arm, working the muscles loose from the long period of immobility.

For nearly all the time Chase took pictures, she'd barely noticed anything more than mild discomfort. Nothing she couldn't handle. But now with her mind racing, and Murphy's hands working her muscles, her skin felt prickly and painful. On top of that, the shame of sitting on his soft leather pants with no barrier from her pussy drove her a little crazy. When he finally moved her off him, he would see her shame in all its wetness ruining his expensive pants.

"You're worrying too much."

"No — No I'm fine," she lied.

"Uh-huh. Don't think for a second just because I'm not looking at your face that I can't feel every emotional response in your body language. Not to mention the increasing tension in these muscles."

Murphy had moved on to her left arm, and while his strong fingers felt incredibly good on her skin, it wasn't her arms that needed his attention.

"Lean back," he whispered at her ear, the warm air caressing her skin.

Eve hesitated. She wanted to go home. She needed to curl up in her own bed, with her own thoughts, and figure out what had gone wrong. Why Chase had turned away from her.

The hands wrapped around her biceps tightened and pulled her back. Eve didn't want to fight. Still, when she leaned against his chest she didn't relax. She held part of her weight away from him with the use of her stomach muscles.

Thwap! Murphy slapped her thigh, catching her completely off guard. She gasped at the stinging heat spreading through her leg.

"Stop trying to hold yourself back from me, Eve. That's not how this works." That stern in-command voice had returned and Eve swore she literally felt some of her resistance melting away. She sighed into him, giving in to the need to be close. In a few minutes she would compose herself and go home, but for now she would take advantage of what he offered and asked for. Besides, he'd begun working his magical fingers on her hips, thighs, and belly. Maybe there was hope for that orgasm after all. Certainly the need for release was what had her guts twisted in a knot.

Before long, he'd created a state of euphoria in her that led her to a point halfway between the need pulsing between her legs and the almost overpowering desire to sleep. Then his hands touched her breasts and the simmering flame leaped to a small fire.

"I know, Eve, I know. There isn't a doubt in my mind about what you need. But you have walls. Thick ones that you need to let down. So, until you're ready to tell us what you want, really tell us, you can't have it."

His thumb and forefinger pressed on her sensitive nipples at the end of his statement, and Eve cried out. Not from pain. No, she loved the way he gently tormented her. Her cries had to do with her inability to voice the need they'd created in her. She jumped from Murphy's lap, her embarrassment briefly lost in the face of her desire to escape.

"I have to go." She grabbed her clothes from the floor and rushed to the dressing room without a glance back at Murphy. Once there, she closed and locked the door and hurriedly dressed. The quicker she got out, the quicker she could make sense of what had happened today.

Five minutes later Eve unlocked and opened the door a fraction, looking to see if Murphy had followed her. When she saw no one, she breathed a sigh of relief. He'd obviously decided to let her go. She opened the door, rushed to her desk, and grabbed her purse.

Now all she had to do was make it out the door without either one of them catching her and she'd be home free.

"Where are you going?"

Shit.

She didn't want to turn around and face Chase. Not yet. Until she had her emotions under control, she was entirely too vulnerable. After an hour with her battery-operated boyfriend and about eight hours of sleep, then maybe she'd be up to it. But now? No way.

"I'm going home for the night." She did her best to hide the quaver in her voice and prayed he'd leave it at that.

Chase grabbed her arm and led her down the corridor toward the exit without another word. At the door, he backed her into the wall and bracketed her face with his hands. He seared her clear down to her soul with the hunger in his gaze before lowering his lips to hers. With the angry demeanor and the tense lines she'd seen on his face, she expected a rough taking of her mouth. Wanted it even.

Instead his lips slid across hers softly, sending shivers of sensation straight to her stomach and other warm places in her body. He took the time to taste and learn before his tongue dipped inside, coaxing her mouth open. The deeper he went, the weaker Eve felt, until her knees wobbled and she thought her legs would give out.

The warm, soothing kiss acted like a balm to her frazzled nerves. She'd begun to tumble into a well of helplessness after leaving Murphy as she recalled everything she'd endured. Although *endured* hardly suited how she'd felt. Everything they'd done made her want more until no matter what they did it wasn't enough.

Now this kiss…

Chase delved deeper, increasingly forceful, until he'd begun to devour her where she stood. Tongue and teeth worked in tandem to rob her senses while he staked a claim. What else could you call something so intense, so fraught with need, moisture flooded between her legs?

The inferno blazing inside her raged out of control. Thoughts of begging pushed at her brain. She grabbed at his waist. The need to be close — to have more of him — melted through her fear. When she thought she couldn't take another second more before she combusted, he jerked back and out of her reach.

"Jesus, Eve." He clenched his fingers in his hair and looked away.

Fresh tears pooled in her eyes, but they held no comparison to the painful need throbbing between her thighs. "Touch me, Chase…" Her legs shook out of control. "I need more…"

Eve slipped her hand beneath her skirt. Trembling fingers slid along the soaking-wet flesh. "I swear it won't take much. One touch…"

Chase grabbed her wrist and yanked it away from her pussy. The dark look in his eyes was like molten lava to her insides.

"No." He placed her arm above her head and locked it in place with a tight grip. "If this is going to keep going, you need to learn right now that your pleasure will only come from Murphy or me. Never your own hand unless we've directed it."

Eve cried out and squirmed against his hold. She was ready to crawl up his body like a cat in heat if that's what it took. What the hell was pride at this point anyway?

Chase kissed his way from the edge of her shoulder to the shell of her ear while he caressed the inside of her thigh with his free hand mere inches from where she desperately needed him to be. But it was the rock-hard ridge pushing into her hip that commanded her attention. He was as turned on as she.

"Don't touch your pussy tonight," he whispered, the sound an unmistakable command. "You started this and I plan to finish it. When you're ready." Chase chose that moment to drag one finger through her slit. Eve cried out from the overload of sensation. Her knees buckled. Thanks to the strong grip he maintained on her arm, she stayed right where he wanted her.

"Please..." She couldn't have held back the plea if she'd wanted to. She'd known Chase and Murphy would play her body like a finely tuned instrument, but she'd underestimated her own response. Now she needed an orgasm as much as her next breath, and he'd just denied her.

"I intend to give you everything you need and then some." He removed his finger and released her arm, and Eve barely caught herself from falling. "But not tonight."

Eve had no idea what to do with that. The ache bordered on painful, and he'd just ordered her no satisfaction. Was he fucking crazy? As quickly as a flash fire in a pan of grease on the stove, her aching desire turned to anger.

"You're being such an asshole. Is it really all that much to ask for some relief? Fuck, Chase. Have some pity."

The smug smile that crossed his face fanned the flames. She suddenly wanted to knock that look from his face.

"Consider this a test. Or a last chance to say no if you need that. I could send the client the pictures we have already and I think he'd be more than pleased, although there were a few more shots I wanted to get tomorrow." He took a step forward, putting her within arm's reach again. "I'm not doing this to punish you. You were incredible today. But right now I need you to trust me. If you touch that pretty little cunt of yours tonight, don't come in. You can take the day off with pay and return to your former position on Monday. No harm, no foul."

With that he turned and walked in the direction of his office. No rebuttal permitted, no allowing her a response. Nothing. She slid to the floor, finally allowing the tears she'd held back to drip down her cheeks. With Chase gone, her emotions crashed down on her. Panic at the thought of Murphy or Chase finding her like that gripped her insides and pushed her to her feet. Home. She had to get there.

She was now certain she'd bitten off more than she expected and that any sane woman would leave and never return. By the same token she knew without a single doubt she'd return in the morning.

SIX

Chase stared at the images on his computer screen. He'd worked endlessly on these shots since he'd walked away from Eve. And walking away from her had been one of the hardest things he'd ever done. He'd seen the hurt in her eyes—the desperate need. The second he'd closed his office door he'd licked his finger clean. Not the smartest thing he'd ever done. Since then her taste and smell was all he'd thought of for the past nine hours.

He'd known going down this road would not be smart, and the minute he'd focused on her through his lens, the war was over. At least for him. There would be no more denial of what he wanted from Eve. The rock-hard erection in his pants proved that.

No, little Miss Eve would be his. Plain and simple. He'd offered her more than a fair share of outs, even though he'd known she wouldn't take them. If he'd had a doubt of her intentions before, these pictures cleared up everything. Her words could lie, desire could tempt her where she didn't really need to go, but the camera, it never lied.

There in the photos lay the perfect submissive. His submissive. Funny how life threw things at you when you least expected it. She'd stumbled into his life on a whim without a lick of secretarial experience, and Murphy had taken her in.

"Fuck, Chase. Have you been here all night again?"

Before he could respond, a white foam box landed on his desk, disturbing the organized chaos he had going on.

"Do you really expect me to answer that?" Chase popped open the box and sighed at the gourmet omelet from his favorite all-night café. He hadn't thought of anything other than Eve for so many hours that he'd forgotten to eat, and now his stomach growled furiously for sustenance.

"See, there is a God. And he called up you, Murphy Young, to deliver me the finest food I've seen in too long." Chase grabbed the plastic silverware and ripped into the bag it came in. He freed the fork and dug into the food. The fluffy egg and cheese crossed his taste buds in a ridiculously delightful experience. "Oh yeah, now that's what I'm talking about."

"You should try leaving the office every once in a while. You might be surprised by what you find out there." Murphy settled into the leather couch across from his desk and placed his feet on the coffee table.

"Yeah, fuck you too."

Rich laughter erupted from his best friend and provider of decent food. "So, I take it you like the shots from yesterday."

"You tell me." He grabbed up one of the 8 x 10s he'd already printed in high resolution and handed it over.

Chase knew the instant Murphy's facial expression turned serious, he'd been right. He'd captured some of his best work with Eve. Once she'd given in to the bindings, everything about her had begun to change. A low whistle from the couch shook Chase from his thoughts and brought his attention back to Murphy.

"This is pretty unbelievable. And why do I have a sudden hunch we're not getting paid enough for these photos?" Murphy handed the photo back to Chase, who stared into the eyes of the woman he craved more than ever. The combination of fear, lust, and crazy want in her gaze tore into his gut every time he looked.

"What happened when she left? Please tell me you talked to her."

"Yeah I talked to her all right, but she was pretty damn pissed at me the last time I saw her."

"Chaaase." The exasperated sound of Murphy's voice when he spoke his name amused him. If his friend didn't know him by now, he never would. "You were mean to her, weren't you?"

He couldn't tear his gaze from her photo. Her skin practically glowed against the ropes. Full breasts topped with the perfect bright red nipples drew his attention here, almost as much as they did in person. Oh what he could do with tits like those.

"Are you even listening to me?" Murphy asked.

"Yeah, I hear you just fine."

"Then what the hell? I know you've had a bug up your ass since she started working here, but looking at those photos and after her performance yesterday, I thought you'd be thrilled."

Chase slammed down the picture and turned a hard look to his friend. "That's exactly the problem, isn't it? It's not a performance. Our little receptionist has a submissive streak a mile wide."

"Even better." Murphy sat up straight and placed his feet on the floor. "You've been out of the play scene for too long, and it's high time you got on with finding someone new."

"Don't try to force this on me. I won't put up with bullshit like that."

Murphy barked in laughter. "Force you. Are you fucking kidding me? Your tongue was practically hanging out when I walked in here, and don't think I missed your reactions yesterday.

You want her bad. So what exactly is the problem?"

"You know, you can go now. I do still have some more work to do this morning, just in case our new protégée decides to show up."

"What do you mean? Why wouldn't she? Did you purposely try to scare her off again last night?"

Chase rolled his eyes and stood. Movement. He needed movement. Murphy grilling him about Eve was getting under his skin. "I was truthful, goddammit, so quit giving me shit about it. If Eve comes in today, it won't just be for pictures."

Murphy half smiled at him. "Did you even bother to explain why we held her back from the orgasm she begged for?"

He kept silent. He didn't have to answer to Murphy if he didn't want to. They were business partners first, play partners second. Although the fact they'd been best friends since childhood probably superseded it all.

"You are one hard man, Chase. Even I couldn't have resisted her soft pleas for a second more. If I'd held her for two minutes longer, that hot cunt of hers would have been in my mouth. It's all I thought about last night after I went home. I mean, hell, don't even ask how many times I had to jack off in order to fall asleep."

"You know if she obeyed, and kept her hands away from herself, the pictures I'll get today will be off the fucking charts. I really might have to ask the client for more." Chase paced across the room and willed his hands to stay at his sides. The zipper pressing against his engorged dick was going to leave marks. But if he expected her to exercise control, then he'd sure do the same. It was the least he could do.

"You're waiting for her, aren't you?" Murphy looked at him with a narrowed gaze. "Yep, I can see it. The Chase Miller legendary control is hard at work and clawing up your back, isn't it?"

"I need her to come back."

Murphy sighed deeply. "She'll be back, and we both know it. Hell, I hope so. I've never experienced anyone quite like her. I know she's not completely innocent, but she has a quality about her. Someone just needs to work through her control issues. It's no wonder she's so curious about bondage. Nothing like a little forced helplessness to bring out the inner slut we're looking for."

An idea crawled into Chase's head, and he hurried back to his desk. He sank into the deep leather chair and swiveled to the computer. The photo he'd been manipulating for the last few hours haunted him. With a computerized paintbrush, he painted on four simple letters and sat back to look at the results.

"What do you think?"

Murphy launched himself from the sofa and crossed the room. He peered over Chase's shoulder and absorbed the last photo he'd taken. Now emblazoned with the word *slut*.

"Perfect. It suits her to a tee." The approval in Murphy's voice was unmistakable. No wonder they did everything so well together. They'd discovered long ago that they were two sides of the same coin. And in this day and age it was all about balance.

"Did you already set up the studio?"

"You know I did."

"Now she just needs to show up." The both glanced at the clock, and Chase frowned. She was already twenty minutes late.

SEVEN

On Chase's last words, Eve slipped around the corner and leaned heavily on the wall. Her heart raced and heat suffused her cheeks, not to mention all the other areas of her body. After a night of very little sleep, worrying over every little thing she'd done wrong, she'd planned to march right into his office and tell him where he could take his attitude and shove it.

Instead she'd overheard Murphy and him having a conversation. Curious, she'd hovered near the door and listened to every word. Every emotion she could think of had slammed through her during the course of the two men talking. She'd been so wrong.

They both wanted her as fiercely as she wanted them. Although from the sound of it, they had pretty high expectations of her. Expectations she wasn't confident she could fulfill. For two years every minute of her life had been about someone else, and she'd somehow lost the ability to let it go. The words relax and go with the flow had left the building. Instead, all she thought about were responsibilities. The work that never ended and the to-do list never more than a few feet from her side.

Even she knew how obsessive that sounded.

Still, every second she stood there her nipples grew tighter and the pulsing in her groin became insistent. Their voices had sounded so excited as they talked about pictures that she was dying to see. The word slut still bounced around in her brain as she tried to decide how she felt about that. It had been spoken irreverently and that shocked her more than the actual word.

But first she needed to stop thinking about touching herself and make an appearance. She could only imagine what Chase might cook up to punish her tardiness. And after what she'd overheard, she was certain it would be something.

Eve lifted from the wall and rose to her full height. Much more than normal thanks to the heels she wore. The red sandals she'd worn today matched the color of her hair exactly, as well as the bra and panty set she'd chosen. God, she loved her shoes and underwear. She might have to admit one day they'd become quite a fetish for her.

She moved toward Chase's office, this time making sure her heels made as much noise as possible. By the time she turned into the doorway, both men stood glaring in her direction.

"You're late." This time the impatience came from Murphy, which startled her. He'd never seemed to care about rules and such.

"Traffic," she lied.

For a few seconds no one said a word, and Eve held her breath. They probably knew she had lied, but she wasn't about to tell them she'd overhead them discussing her. They'd just have to accept her excuse or punish her as they saw fit.

"Looks like today is going to be very interesting, wouldn't you say, Murphy?"

"Looks like it." Murphy reached her in two strides and whispered at her ear, "Did you sleep well, darlin'?"

"Not really." She tried to steady her voice and failed. Having him so close, his warm breath caressed her skin, pebbled her nipples, and short-circuited her brain. God, what would it take to get them to finally have mercy on her?

Simply standing in this room, with Murphy's tall, broad presence almost wrapped around her and Chase watching closely, did something to her feminine core. Her insides melted and the last of the uncertainty and anger she'd dealt with through the night faded away.

"Well, I have a hunch that you're going to get everything you want and then some today. You ready to be a good little girl and pose for Chase's camera?"

She nodded. Butterflies erupted at the thought of more of what they'd given her yesterday. Already she ached to have her arms bound, to be in a position of total reliance on these two virile men.

"Well then, pretty lady, let's you and I head to the studio and get ready. I think Chase mentioned he had some more work to do here."

She glanced at Chase and almost laughed out loud at the way he glared at Murphy. If she hadn't known better, she might have read something more into that. But she knew this was a job. An incredibly sexy, screw-me-to-the-wall-when-we're-done kind of job, but still a job.

Murphy grabbed her hand and led her from the room and away from Chase.

"I haven't checked any of the messages that came in yesterday. Shouldn't I do some of that first?" She prayed he'd say no. The thought of trying to sit at her desk, going about business as usual sounded like the worst possible scenario for her day.

Rope. She wanted to feel Murphy's rough hands sliding across her flesh as he tied her up and had his way with her. Eve swallowed back the groan that would have given her away.

"Nope. Already taken care of. We asked the answering service to field all the calls for a couple of days. So you have nothing to worry about but doing the best you can for the last of these photos. In fact, I should have had Chase show you a couple from yesterday." He held open the door of the studio for her, and she passed underneath his arm. "I think you'll like them. Chase and I think they're incredible."

"Really?" She glanced down at her modest outfit, which did a good job of hiding her flaws and emphasizing some of her assets, like her boobs. She always went for the cleavage. But naked? *Naked* and *incredible* were two words she wouldn't have thought to string together when referring to her appearance.

She didn't hate her body, but she sure as hell didn't live in some denial-warped bubble where she convinced herself she looked as good as their regular models. Lucky for her, plenty of men enjoyed generous curves and a woman who wasn't ashamed of them.

Eve stopped short when she caught sight of the studio changes from yesterday. The couch had been removed and replaced with a bed. A big king-size whopper, covered in red silk sheets. Small tables were added to the side, and one of Chase's erotic prints hung above the headboard. She could imagine between Chase's skill with the camera and his computer software, the photos would look like they'd been taken in a private bedroom versus a photo studio.

"C'mon, don't get nervous on me now." Murphy pulled her closer to the set scene and let go of her hand a couple of feet from the wrought-iron footboard.

The bed looked incredibly heavy, and she wondered where it had come from. All the times she'd peeked in on their shoots, she'd never once seen this scene.

"You like it?" Murphy motioned to the furniture setup. "I found this at an estate sale not too far back, and we've been waiting for the perfect opportunity to use it." He bent over the partition sectioning off the studio and pulled up a coil of black rope. With a wide grin on his face, he made his way back to her. "I think you are the perfect woman to christen this beauty."

A wave of emotion rolled through her at being their first at anything. "It's exquisite. I'd love to have a bed like that in my place." Absentmindedly she reached for the iron and brushed her fingers across the cool metal curve. Tracing the patterns of the ironwork like she would a potential lover.

"An estate sale?" She couldn't picture him scouring through estate and attic sales looking for treasures. But it made sense given their profession. Not every client wanted the traditional dungeon or industrial scene. And they certainly aimed to please.

"Take off your clothes, Eve." His quiet demand flashed through her quick and hot. Getting lost in her thoughts about decorating, she'd momentarily forgotten why she was here. She turned away from the bed and faced him fully. She'd already bought into the assignment, and they'd seen everything she had yesterday, so there wasn't a reason in the world to be shy today. One button at a time she revealed more and more of her skin, and in a way, of herself. If this last day of shooting was all she'd ever have, then she'd damn sure squeeze every ounce out of it that she could.

Staring into Murphy's eyes, she watched them darken in appreciation as she swiftly removed her shirt. She'd gone for a shelf bra that merely hugged the undercurve of each breast and left her nipples uncovered and available. As much as she might like to blame the fact her nipples were already hard on the temperature of the room, they probably both knew better.

"Mmm. It's a shame we have to take that off. But I'm going to remember that sexy bra, 'cause I'm going to want to see that again." Eve lifted her arms and unclasped the hook and eye fasteners behind her back and let the lacy garment fall away. As much as she wanted to see more of Murphy in the future, she knew enough to take everything he said with a grain of salt. Some of it had to be about the scene.

"Do you have something specific you want me to wear for today?"

"As a matter of fact, I do. But we'll save that surprise for later." His gaze traveled down the plane of her body, from her face all the way to the tips of her toes. "I really do like those shoes though, so let's keep those on. Unless Chase says something else, those are staying on." She looked down at the brand new peep toe heels with black lace overlaid across cream silk. She'd nearly fallen to her knees to thank the shoe Gods when she'd found these beauties. The corners of her lips curved into a small smile. He had no idea how much that pleased her. What more could a shoe fetishist ask for?

She reached behind her once again and unzipped the long, slim skirt she'd worn. With a couple of tugs, the fabric pooled at her feet, and she softly stepped away from the garment. When she bent to retrieve it, hot hands touched the bared flesh of her ass.

"Holy shit, woman. You really don't make it easy to keep a mind on the job, do you? A G-string and those fucking shoes? I swear I've died and gone to heaven."

Eve couldn't speak or move. The rough feel of his big, strong hands stroking her backside robbed her of breath. Whatever happened, she desperately didn't want him to stop. In slow motion, he pushed a couple of fingers under the skimpy fabric and peeled it down her legs all the way to the floor.

"Step out," he instructed. Eagerly, she complied. Free of the lingerie, she moved to stand, and a firm hand at the back of her waist held her in the bent-over position. "Uh-uh. Not yet."

Eve stilled and held her breath. There was something insanely arousing about standing vulnerable and open to a man like this. Especially one as dominant as Murphy. The weight of his hand holding her down might as well have been him touching her clit for the pleasure it gave her. He stroked down her flank and the back of her thighs, sending heat and fire streaking to all of her erogenous zones. Before she could recover her wits, both hands grabbed the flesh of her globes and spread her backside apart.

"Spread your legs." A booted foot nudged at her ankle. A little shocked to be in this position, Eve moved her feet to a wider stance, opening herself even farther. The leg Murphy had wedged between her thighs moved deeper until the fabric of his pants nudged at her pussy. She gasped and dug her teeth into her bottom lip. It was too soon to beg. Based on what she'd heard in Chase's office, there'd be no relief to the burning need now swelling her clit.

"I'd like a picture just like this. The pretty girl with sexy shoes bent over with her ass open and ready. I'd stare at a picture like that every night and dream about which hole I wanted to fill first." He loosened the grip of one hand and a thick finger slid along her slit. "And wet too. Very nice."

Jesus, he really was going to kill her. Eve fought to stay perfectly still when everything in her brain demanded she move against him. Only one touch of the blunt tip of his finger against her clit and she'd get off and her torture would finally be over. Instead the long digit moved to her entrance and tickled the opening.

"Murphy...please don't."

His movements halted. "You don't want me to touch you today?"

"Of course I do. But I'm going out of my mind. All this teasing. I've never—I can't take it." Not without going out of her fucking mind anyway.

"Don't worry too much, little one. Your wait is almost over." He released her abruptly and Eve had to grab on to the railing of the bed to keep from toppling over. "I'll give you a short respite, how's that?"

Eve nodded. Her vocal cords didn't want to work. Only her tear ducts seemed in perfect order these last twenty-four hours.

"Stand up, then, and let's get you tied up." Her stomach clenched. Not with I'm-scared nerves, but the oh-my-God-I-can't-wait kind.

She stood on shaky legs and turned to Murphy's voice. The smile from earlier had disappeared and had been replaced with the serious look of a man ready to work.

"We aren't doing anything complex today. This client likes to see a girl tied up but doesn't particularly care about anything too fancy. He's definitely not a shibari kind of guy." He lifted the rope and wrapped it around the back of her head. With the two loose ends dangling between her breasts, he lifted her hair and made sure none of it remained trapped underneath.

She'd seen many examples of his work with the incredible art of Japanese rope bondage. He practiced a lot, and more than once he'd called her in to the studio to show off his latest feat. Every single time she'd felt a jolt to her stomach and wished he'd try using her for a model one time.

He got a lot of regular phone calls requesting his services, and the word around the studio was that many submissives offered themselves to him in service on a regular basis. Of course she had no clue how many he took up on their offers. He and Chase remained intensely close-mouthed about any time they spent in their favorite club, Purgatory. Once, she'd gone so far as to call the club to inquire about private dungeon membership, but to her dismay had learned that not only would she be required to have a sponsor, the fees were far outside her budget.

Murphy's warm hands brushed underneath her breasts as he twisted the rope under and over them. After one pass, she realized he was making a rope halter that would leave her breasts exposed but tied tightly enough they would bulge a little at the bindings.

"Can you breathe okay like that? I want it to be tight, but I need you to let me know if it's more than you can bear." Tight was an understatement.

"I'll be fine." At least for now. Lastly he wrapped the rope back around her neck and looped it between her breasts with one final wrap underneath before tying it off in the back. He took a few steps back and admired his work.

"Not bad, if I do say so myself." He circled around her. "You need one more thing, but we'll wait till the last minute for that. On your knees, beautiful."

Her hesitation only lasted a few seconds, but by the dark cloud that suddenly settled across his face...he noticed.

Eve sank to her knees not only because she'd been ordered to, but because she wanted to. A command from him or Chase sent a dark thrill into her hungry soul. She adjusted her feet and legs so that her shoes didn't affect her comfort. Although her comfort was not of utmost importance at the moment.

Oh no.

Murphy had moved off the small set to a wardrobe and immediately removed his jeans. As he rifled through the clothes hanging inside the cabinet, she was left with the most spectacular view she'd ever seen. His naked backside.

Obviously he went commando or she'd have noticed him removing underwear. The tight shape of his ass nearly made her swallow her tongue. Lean, muscular legs that flexed as he moved caught her eye, and she couldn't look away. Not even when he pulled a pair of black dress pants over them.

Quickly Eve checked to see if her mouth stood open, because openly drooling would surely embarrass the hell out of her when he caught her. With those powerful legs out of sight, she studied his back and the tattoo that covered it. The tribal markings took up nearly every inch of his back, and the intricate designs mesmerized her with every movement he made. One of these days she'd ask him what they meant. She didn't know him as well as she'd like, but she knew him enough to know that whatever he'd permanently marked his gorgeous skin with would have meaning.

Unfortunately he dragged a white dress shirt over all those gorgeous muscles and cut off her view. Still she watched him dress, fascinated with the care he took with his appearance. From the perfectly tucked-in shirt, to the rag he grabbed to polish the dress shoes before he slid them on his feet. The man moved with such grace and style, she couldn't help but be impressed.

Finally he grabbed a jacket and untied bow tie and headed her way.

"Enjoy the show?" His lips twitched.

"Yes, I did."

"Probably not as much as I enjoyed mine." Before she could respond, the studio door opened and a slice of bright sunshine cut through the darkened room. Chase walked in with two cameras wrapped around his neck and a manila folder in his hand.

"Looks like the two of you are about ready. Thought you might like to see these before we got started." He walked straight to her and offered her the packet he carried.

Eve accepted the file and opened it. Nothing could have prepared her for the image. Stark, real, beautiful, lust—so many words popped into her mind as she sifted through them. Chase was a genius with a camera. Never in her life had she looked like this.

"Oh my God, Chase. These are unbelievable. How did you do this? How did you make me look so..." Tears of joy sprang in her eyes and rolled down her cheeks.

Chase knelt in front of her, letting his camera fall to his chest. He stroked his thumbs across her face and wiped away the moisture. "Beautiful."

The simple word sparked a tumultuous wave of overwhelming emotion. She threw her arms around his neck and jumped into his lap. "Thank you. Thank you. Thank you." She peppered his neck with kisses, marveling at the warmth and gratitude she felt for him.

"I guess she likes them."

Eve turned and stared at Murphy. "Like them? I love them. I'm amazed. I knew how exceptional your photos were, but these…" She had no words for how incredible they made her feel.

"I'm glad you like them." Chase placed her back on her knees. "Now we need to finish. You ready?"

Eve nodded. Nerves erupted in her stomach at the last look Chase gave her before turning away. Somehow in that one glance he managed to convey so much heat she nearly burned up from it. The newly formed lump in her throat prevented her from speaking, which was probably just as well. There was nothing important to be said at this point.

The three of them had a job to do. Something that would lead her into a path of temptation that would surely drive her crazy if she wasn't careful. As long as it wasn't her heart involved, she'd be fine.

Eve squeezed her eyes tight against the thought. Those were not ideas she'd allow herself to entertain. No more heartache. She couldn't get involved beyond this photo shoot. She had responsibilities that required her full attention, and being distracted temporarily was one thing. Beginning to think she might want a longer-term submissive role with either Chase or Murphy was such a bad idea.

"Open your eyes, darling." Murphy moved to the velvet love seat she knelt next to and took a seat a few inches out of sight behind her. Didn't change the fact that his energy stirred the air around them. If her pussy wasn't already soaked in anticipation from the day before, it sure as hell was now.

His knee touched her back, and her breath caught in her throat. She wanted so much right now, her body pulsed with it. Eve tracked Chase's movements across the room as he flipped on the built-in stereo controls. Sharp music with an industrial background filled the studio.

"Don't focus on the music. Let the beat be the background as you pay attention to me and my directions." Murphy's breath brushed through her hair, so close to her ear. A shudder raced down her spine. "Eyes on Chase, but it's my voice that will command you today. Do you understand?"

"Yes," she whispered.

"Yes what?"

"Yes, Sir." The dynamic from yesterday had definitely changed. Already the power from

Murphy enveloped her in a tight embrace she desperately craved. Then Chase was squatting a few feet in front of her, his camera already covering his face, waiting for the perfect shot.

A warm hand cupped her breast. Eve sighed and arched her back into the touch. Chase could take all the pictures he wanted. She didn't care as long as Murphy didn't stop. *God, please don't let him stop. Have to have more*. Her breath came in small pants, her mouth opening for air.

"That's it, baby. Show Chase how much you love my touch." Two fingers closed around her already beaded nipple and began a slow and steady squeeze. The pressure arced through her, shooting streaks of pleasure to every limb. Even when the pressure became painful, it wasn't enough.

"More." A low chuckle sounded from behind her.

"Don't worry, little girl. You are going to get so much more today."

Suddenly the sweet ache at her nipple turned to a fiery pinch. She gasped and whimpered, her mind registering the intense pain and ordering her to stop it. Her hands moved to fix it.

"Don't you fucking move." Taken aback by the harsh command from Murphy, Eve froze.

He encircled her throat with one hand and gently squeezed, all the while his fingers tightened on that same nipple. Tears sprang to her eyes, and she fought to keep herself under control. When she didn't think she could hold her position one second longer, Murphy released her nipple, and the sharp pain worsened as blood rushed back into the tip. *Jesus H. Christ.*

Arousal spiked in her clit. Juices trickled between her thighs. Eve wiggled her ass, her only goal to create more friction between her legs.

"Stop." Murphy's hand tightened on her neck. She froze. A sliver of fear broke through the need building in her cunt. "Another move like that and you'll find yourself strung up to the ceiling with my belt burning your pretty little flesh."

Eve took the threat with the seriousness in which it had been delivered. For whatever reason the Dom voice had taken over, and she didn't doubt a word Murphy spoke. She hated the fact she couldn't see his eyes. Would she find anger? Or maybe lust. God she needed to see him.

For a brief second she noticed the camera practically in her face as Chase moved around her. Until Murphy yanked her toward him, and her back arched across his knees. He'd not released his grip, but she trusted he would know if she had trouble breathing. As it was, she was only able to take short, shallow breaths with that much pressure on her windpipe.

"Don't be a bad girl, Eve. As much fun as it would be to punish you, I have better ideas for what we can do with our time. Don't you?"

Fuck yeah. She could reach for her clit and with one stroke get herself off. That's how on edge they had her.

"I can see the wheels turning in there. Is your pussy aching to be touched? I know my dick is rock hard and throbbing to be inside you." Eve's mouth watered. She'd loved giving head yesterday and would gladly take a cock in her mouth again if that's what he wanted. Anything he wanted, she would do.

Please. She mouthed the word but didn't have enough breath to be heard. Murphy bent closer until his lips barely touched hers.

"I know. Me too." His lips crashed down on hers, his fingers loosening their hold around her windpipe. She opened her mouth and his tongue dived in, seeking hers. The urgent pressure of the kiss tore through her, stealing what little air she had left. This was no sweet kiss. No, it had become a taking in every sense of the word. All teeth, lips, and tongue fighting for dominance. Eve kissed him back, her body going crazy for more of this man. She'd never forget this kiss in a million years.

The moment he released his grip on her throat, she wanted to cry out for him to not stop. It dawned on her that she hadn't been frightened at all. She'd been excited and more aroused than she'd ever remembered.

Finally, his mouth released her, and they sat immobile for a few minutes, simply staring at each other. They both breathed heavily, and the rush of power swirling around her offered a sense of possession. Maybe even owned, if only in that brief moment in time. With her head resting on his thighs, she wanted to melt into him. To be a part of everything he needed in that moment. The here and now meant everything to her.

"Spread your knees."

She quickly complied and spread them as wide as she could without breaking eye contact. The music trembled through her system, and the faint clicking of the camera sounded in the back of her mind. Chase wasn't forgotten, but instead of being nervous or afraid of his camera, she wanted him to see her like this. To capture this extreme moment of pride and pleasure she felt.

Murphy's hand traced her collarbone from one side to the other, a light teasing motion that bordered on tickling. Goose bumps rose on her skin, and he grinned down at her.

"I like you like this. All soft and open. Willing. That's the word I'd call it. Are you willing, Eve?"

"Yes, Sir." She bit her bottom lip to control the wide smile threatening to break out. He trailed his fingers to her breasts, but maintained the featherlight touch. She ached for a heavy hand, but he was in control and she was here to simply please him.

He skimmed farther down her torso, where he circled and dipped a fingertip into her belly button.

"God, do you have any idea how delicious these curves look?" A jolt streaked through her stomach then. A silly reminder that she needed to be careful here. If she gave herself fully to these men, she might not make it back. She couldn't afford to lose herself. She had to hold on to a piece of control.

A strong finger slipped between the folds of her sex, only glancing across her swollen bud. Her body jerked, and she gasped from the fleeting pleasure. Already he'd moved on to the opening where he teased and circled. Eve canted her hips, eager for him to dip inside. To fuck her with his finger like he wanted to with his dick.

The sudden image of him thrusting in and out of her aching sex proved her undoing. She whimpered with the need of it. Instead, his fingers spread her lips wide and the clicking of the damned camera sounded nonstop. She couldn't—wouldn't—tear her eyes from Murphy, but every instinct warned that Chase was documenting every curve and fold more thoroughly than any doctor ever had.

Unbidden, a giggle slipped from her lips before she could stop it.

"You finding this funny?"

"He's taking close-ups, isn't he?"

Murphy smiled wickedly at her. "Maybe."

She should have laughed, but despite the curve of his luscious mouth, the serious heat shining in his eyes clogged her throat and made her think of sex again. Fuck the camera. Someone needed to fuck *her* already.

"I need to come, Sir."

"I know you do." That wasn't the response she'd been hoping for. Although he did stop holding her open and went back to massaging the tender skin of her pussy.

He rubbed harder, and the friction heated her through. Her brain fogged up, and she didn't have clear thoughts anymore. "It's not time for you to come yet, little girl. You're still holding back. Tell me why?"

Eve tried to focus on his question, but she couldn't. Every thought and impulse in her body was centered on her needy clit and her pulse beating through it. She pushed her hips against his hand and wiggled her bottom. He rubbed harder but remained firmly away from the one spot she wanted. Her cries of frustration filled the room, and Murphy only smiled down at her.

"No matter how hard you try, you won't come until I tell you to. I will control everything today, not you. Feel that. Think about it. Let it wrap around you like a warm blanket." His fingers slipped a few inches higher, and she nearly exploded when they finally hit the place she needed them to be.

Lightning quick, her body tensed for the oncoming orgasm. He rubbed harder. "You will not come yet, Eve. I have not given permission."

"What? Oh no. Please, Murphy, Sir. I can't hold it back. Please let me."

"No," he commanded loudly. Still he rubbed even stronger. No way would she be able to stop the inferno raging through her.

"I'm going to come. Please—Oh God—I can't—Stop!"

Murphy stopped rubbing and grabbed her clit in a vise-tight grip between two fingers. Sudden pain sliced through her. Her release froze, teetering on a cliff. "Pinch your nipple," he ordered.

Eve grabbed the opposite nipple from the tender one he'd worked before and squeezed.

"Oh c'mon, be serious. I said pinch it."

She pressed harder.

"More."

Again she increased the pressure until the combination of pain between clit and nipple rivaled each other. When the pain reached the crescendo of her tolerance, something odd happened. Her mind went into overdrive, everything fell away, and a cloud of softness settled over her.

She floated on the edges of her mind. No longer in any pain. *Safe*. That's the word she was looking for. A comfortable, happy safeness she'd never felt before.

"There you go. So beautiful. Such joy on your face. Even better than an orgasm." Eve didn't know what was going on, but she still wanted more. She needed Murphy to keep going. As if he'd read her mind, he bent his head to her skin and bit into her flesh. Little sharp bites on her neck that sent her soaring even further.

"Get her to the bed." She vaguely heard Chase's voice in the background. Murphy removed his mouth from her skin, and she cried out in protest.

"Shhh. Trust me, Eve. It's about to get even better." He shifted her body and scooped her into his arms, lifting her from the ground. Her legs ached a little, but it seemed unimportant. The music grew louder, and she let the steady beat flow through her. She liked the tune, even though she had no idea what it was.

Murphy laid her on the pretty red silk sheets where she gasped at the cool touch on her flaming-hot skin. She'd grown incredibly sensitive to everything.

"Lie back and raise your arms over your head and grab the hook there." She listened to Murphy give her instructions, fascinated with the movement of his lush lips. She did as he asked and grabbed on to the smooth, round metal that reminded her of a giant eyehook.

While she'd gotten lost in her thoughts, Murphy had grabbed some more of the strong black rope and now stood over her, wrapping her wrists. It dawned on her that in everything that had gone on thus far, she'd completely forgotten about the rope halter still tied around her body, despite the tight pull she got from it every time she moved. Now she wanted more. She liked the snug, safe feel of it and wondered what her whole body would feel like wrapped up tight by Murphy.

"Spread your legs." She opened her legs, and cool air brushed against her sex. A new ache bloomed for more of Murphy's touch. God. He needed to stop torturing her already.

"Will you fuck me now?" She could hardly wait. Murphy and Chase both laughed as together they shackled her legs with the leather ankle restraints she'd noticed earlier.

"She's pretty eager." Chase's smooth voice flowed over her like warm oil. She wanted to rub him in and keep him forever.

"What'd you expect after we primed her yesterday and then tormented her more today?"

"It's incredible seeing her like this. I expected more resistance." All she heard was the modulated tones of Chase's voice teasing her senses. Resist him? Was he crazy?

"Please fuck me," she begged. If that's what they wanted, she'd happily give them that.

"Fuck, Chase. Hurry."

"Then get out of the way. I only need a few minutes." Murphy moved out of her sight, and Chase picked up his camera again. "Tell me how you feel, Eve. Show me."

"Show you how? I can barely move."

"Then tell me."

"I need to be fucked. I'm so horny I can't stand it."

"I already know that. Tell me something I don't know." Chase's camera clicked away as he spoke to her.

"I—uh—I feel so different."

"Different how?" Why did he keep grilling her instead of touching her? Tears pricked at the back of her eyes, and she feared she might start crying again.

"I don't know. Just different."

"C'mon Eve, I know you can do this. I only need a few more pictures. You're incredible like that. All tied up, dying to be fucked. Does it hurt?"

"No, not exactly." Did it hurt? No. "It's like pressure. You've taken my ability to move away, yet I feel safer than ever."

"Why do you trust us?"

Trust? The word hadn't even entered her consciousness yet.

"I don't know. What do you want from me, Chase? It's hard to think straight. All I can think about is Murphy biting my neck again. Or you filling me with your cock. Someone, hurting me."

Chase froze, lowering his camera. "What did you say?"

Eve racked her brain. What had she said? Chase unhooked the camera from around his neck. He walked around the side of the bed and set the camera down on the table.

"Why do you need this, Eve? If you can tell me that, then I promise to give you everything you want and more."

"What?"

"Tell me. Don't think about it. Don't ask me questions. Tell me." He wrapped his hand around a breast and stroked across a nipple. Automatically her hands jerked, but they were tied securely to the bed.

"I'm scared, Chase."

"Scared of what?" He bent to her, his mouth hovering dangerously close to a tight nipple. "You may not know why, but you can trust us. You can't hold back. You have to give to us everything you need. We demand it. I demand it."

A tear pooled at the corner of her eye before slowly sliding down the side of her cheek. Chase noticed and shifted his position, his face leaning into hers. He licked at the solitary tear.

"Please, Chase. I have to come. It hurts so much."

"I thought you wanted to hurt," he teased. Strong fingers blazed a heated trail to her saturated sex and delved between the folds. He pushed two inside her, thrusting deep before slowly dragging them back out. Eve watched, mesmerized as he brought those glistening fingers to his mouth. Her thighs clenched painfully while he licked every drop of her juice from his skin.

"She's ready." In the blink of an eye, Murphy returned to the bed, already naked. His cock jutted from his hips, long, thick, and weeping at the slit with precum. She was more than willing to go through with this, yet she couldn't stop the flutter of nerves in her stomach if she tried. He tore at the condom he carried and tossed the foil to the ground. Two seconds later he was sheathed and prodding her entrance with the tip of his shaft. Rubbing it up and down her slit, teasing her.

She groaned, and Chase swallowed her cry with his mouth. Slow and easy he pushed his tongue between her lips and devoured her mouth. Every time he kissed her like this she couldn't fight the sense that this wasn't normal for him. Or maybe it wasn't her who was normal when all she could think about was the vivid connection she felt when he kissed her like this.

Their tongues tangled while Murphy remained at her entrance, only rubbing her. She was certain she was going to combust or explode into a thousand pieces before they ever stopped withholding.

The kiss deepened, and Chase moved his hands everywhere. He grabbed her shoulders; he scratched his nails lightly down her chest and across her tits. The exquisite pleasure of his touch combined with the faint streak of pain he added to his movements flooded her already overloaded mind. His hands wrapped around her waist, and she arched in his direction eager for him to scratch at her back if he wanted. Instead he traveled upward and grabbed two handfuls of her hair and pulled. Another sharp sting of pain, this one far more intense, coursed through her, giving her a thrill she couldn't get enough of.

It was in that instant when her gaze was locked with Chase, Murphy surged inside her to the hilt. She cried out at the next mind-blowing combination of pain and pleasure as her body stretched to accommodate him.

This is what she needed.

To be taken. To be tied and helpless to whatever they wanted. Not what she wanted. To be forced to endure, to accept, to enjoy everything they wanted her to.

"Good God...Eve!" Murphy's fingers dug into her hips and pressed her into the mattress. Eve suffered such intense arousal it had become painful, and even Murphy's in and out strokes weren't enough.

Chase freed her mouth to explore the sensitive skin of her already aching nipples. The occasional lick was nothing in comparison to the near-constant pressure from his teeth.

Please touch me. She thought the words but that was as far as they got. One flick to her clit and she'd trip and fall over the edge she teetered on. Instead they touched, licked, bit, and fucked everywhere else, ensuring she didn't come until they were good and ready.

If her hands were free, she'd reach down and save herself from their torture. And wait for the punishment after.

Chase released her breasts and pulled back. He attacked the waistband of his jeans, nearly ripping them from his hips. His cock sprang free — thick, long, and hard. Without giving her even a second to say anything, he nudged her mouth open and thrust deep. Eve sucked on him, ecstatic to discover just how needy he'd become. A thrill of satisfaction moved inside her as she lapped the precum leaking from his tip. Salt and man exploded across her taste buds. Greedy as usual, she relaxed her throat and took more of him inch by inch.

Eve tried to hold on to control, but Chase would have none of that. He groaned, placed his hands on the side of her head and began a steady rhythm of driving in and out of her mouth. His control. His taking.

Obviously wanting his fair share of attention, Murphy pinched her clit. The bright, brief moment of bliss flared hot inside her. Not enough to get her off, but she sure as hell came close.

She groaned against Chase's shaft and renewed her efforts to please him to the best of her ability. At the same time she swiveled her hips and contracted her vaginal muscles around Murphy. If she worked hard enough, showed her appreciation enough, then maybe they would finally give in.

EIGHT

Eve moaned again, and Chase smiled. "I think she wants us to put her out of her misery."

"Her misery?" Murphy changed his rhythm and rolled his hips instead of pounding into her. "Try mine. The little minx is trying to milk it out of me."

"I guess we'll have to keep teaching her lessons about who's in control here, then." Chase tightened his hold on her head. "Look at me, darling."

Her glassy gaze turned to his, and he waited for the clouds to clear. "Stop thinking about how desperate your need is. It's our pussy now, and we tell you when you can make it come. We know what you need. Do you understand?"

She blinked and groaned her assent. "If you come before given permission" — he reached down and fingered her clit—"you'll have to be punished. And I don't mean the funishment kind."

Damn, he enjoyed pushing her. She sucked harder, and he wondered what he'd done to deserve her submission. And it was fucking beautiful. Everything about her was. Every time he fisted a handful of hair and tugged, her eyes opened wide and he grabbed her attention. She hummed her pleasure and wriggled against his fingers.

With each driving thrust of his cock, Eve opened wider, allowing him the deepest access to her mouth. "That's it, Eve. Show me how much you want to come."

Her lips firmed around his cock, and the suction she applied increased. With her vigorously working his shaft and the visual of Murphy pounding into her with surprising force, Chase steeled himself for the inevitable loss of control. It was an incredible sight to see Murphy slick with her juices shuttling in and out of her pink flesh. Every new thrust drew another moan from her, sending an electric current straight up his dick. Need seized Chase in a gut-wrenching grip. He added his own moan to the chorus from Murphy and Eve as they rode their way to bliss. For one fleeting moment he thought about this going on forever.

He released her clit and savored the cry of protest vibrating along his dick. Chase couldn't hold out much longer. His balls tightened, and cum boiled hot and ready for an orgasm he knew would blow his mind.

"Come, Eve. Come now!" Chase commanded when he felt his cock swell. Not two seconds later he exploded, shooting streams of cum down her throat. Her eyes slid closed and she swallowed him down, not missing a drop.

Murphy shuddered and shouted, "Fucking A!" as he too lost the fight.

When Eve's orgasm hit, her screams were muffled by his cock still shoved in her mouth. Her eyes rolled back and her face turned serene. The beauty of her pleasure consumed him. A twinge of regret for missing out on her pussy clenching around him flared momentarily. He banked it down and slid from her mouth. He'd have more of her very soon.

Murphy slowly pulled from Eve, removed the condom, and threw it in the trash. Together they sank to the bed, limp and exhausted. Physically Chase was spent, but the turmoil in his mind had increased. They'd finished the photo shoot, and per his instructions it was the end to their scene. So why did his chest ache for more?

He reached for her bound wrists and quickly untied them. The skin was red and slightly chafed. She might have some faint marks the next day, but nothing beyond that. For a few minutes he massaged the tender area, easing the blood flow back to normal. Reluctantly he released her hands, and Eve curled into his embrace, the heat from her body seeping into his weary frame.

Murphy gave him a knowing look as he took up the position against her backside. In a different time or place he might embrace the rightness of this scenario. Instead it brought back memories he didn't want to revisit. He'd thought sharing a woman with Murphy before on a permanent basis had been an ideal situation. With their friendship and business partnership it made sense. Too bad it hadn't lasted. Not only had Cynthia attempted to twist their relationship in a power play, she'd done everything in her power to break the friendship he had with Murphy. They'd both almost lost everything.

Luckily they'd both realized what she was up to and put an end to their ménage before things went too far.

Chase stroked the side of Eve's face, tucking her hair behind her ear. Her eyelids fluttered, but she kept them closed. He sensed she was hovering on the edge of consciousness and deep sleep. They'd put her through a lot in the last two days, and her grit impressed him.

She'd been easy enough to work with for a photo shoot, but would she give her submission so willingly without a paycheck attached to it? Honestly, he didn't doubt her submission, but he'd expected more resistance.

What else would she not fight? He'd had some intense picture ideas lately but had brushed them aside when none of the models seemed to fit what he'd been looking for. Eve, on the other hand... She was the stuff fantasies were made of. Beautiful and curvy, she'd make the perfect retro pinup girl. He'd always had a bit of an obsession with that look. Something to think about, but not exactly what he had in mind at the moment. He wanted to push her submission. To capture the look in her eyes every time he found something new that scared her.

She wasn't a model, so she didn't have a lot of experience. Exactly why the photos they'd already taken were his best ever and why she'd be perfect for what he had in mind.

Damn. It was hard not to think about how perfectly she fit between them. His dick stirred at the thought. He'd let her rest for a while, and then he'd have some more fun.

"Are you thinking what I'm thinking?" Murphy whispered.

Chase tore his gaze from the sleeping Eve and faced his friend. He knew exactly what he thought. He wanted to keep her. Guilt ripped into Chase. He was more than willing to play with her some more, but anything beyond that was out of the question.

"No, Murph. I'm not." He lied because he had to. Giving Murphy false hope was out of the question.

The joy in Murphy's eyes clouded with a dark look. "Well, if you don't want her, then I'll keep her."

Anger moved through Chase before he could consider why. He was not a jealous man, and in fact the thought of photographing the two of them fucking got him half-hard again.

The two of them fucking with him not in the picture just pissed him off.

"We just need to get her out of our system. She's incredibly responsive to us both, and it's been a damn long time."

"You've really turned cold." Murphy didn't wait for a response. He lifted himself from the bed and headed for the door. "Don't be an idiot, Chase. You aren't fooling anyone."

He watched Murphy doing his best to ignore his friend's pain. He'd be back. And in the meantime he had a sweet, warm woman in his bed he really wanted to work with. He suspected they'd barely scratched the surface when it came to her rigid control. He needed to explore her triggers. Dig down and find out why she needed to be restrained to let go and see how much further she'd follow them.

He pressed his lips to her forehead. "Hey, sleepy woman." She sighed at his voice but didn't open her eyes. Usually content with one play scene here and there, Chase realized he wanted more from Eve. Whatever this was might not last long, but he could spend some time with her, teach her to overcome her fears, and give them all some memories to last a lifetime.

Sounded simple enough. If he could just get her awake.

"C'mon, beautiful, wake up."

She stirred restlessly. "I'm awake," she murmured.

"Uh-huh. Sure you are." He pressed his lips to hers, reveling in the soft warmth that greeted him. "I have a proposition for you. But first I need something else."

Chase grabbed her knee and pushed her legs apart, exposing her pussy to his view. The need to be inside her consumed him.

"Chase, what are you doing?"

"I'm still hungry."

Her lips tilted into a half smile, and her lids opened partially. Where he expected to see annoyance or plain exhaustion, he recognized heat and need mirroring his own.

"I'm curious, though..." He trailed kisses along her jawline until she tilted her head back, giving him full access to her neck. Her sighs of pleasure fueled him on. "I'm wondering why you wanted so badly to be tied up. Why were you so willing to volunteer for this assignment when you had no real experience?"

Eve's body tensed. It was as if every muscle contracted at the same time, leaving her stiff as a board. Yeah, he'd hit a nerve all right. When she didn't answer right away, he decided he'd come back to that later if he had to. When her body splayed out for him wasn't such a distraction.

"I like the way it feels." Her answer came on a rough whisper. She may have tensed up, but her desire still burned hotly inside. Good. The more she needed, the more likely he'd get the answers he wanted. She hadn't lied, but there was certainly more to the story.

He trailed his fingers to her chest, where he circled the tightening nipples until they were hard, jutting points. Leaning forward, he licked the irresistible flesh.

One nip and one lick to each breast before he captured one of the tips between his teeth. She arched to him, gasping for breath. Not to bring all the focus on just one, Chase brought his hand to the bare nipple. He twisted and worried it between his fingers in rhythm with his teeth on the other, eliciting a cry from Eve.

"Oh — Chase — more."

Right then he decided teasing and tormenting his little sub would be his new favorite thing to do. Watching her wiggle and worm around on the bed, trying to find the right friction that would get her off, amused the hell out of him.

"Be still," he ordered.

For a moment she froze in place before a firm pinch to her nipple got her moving again. "Be still, or I stop."

That got her attention. She quit wiggling and whimpered her displeasure. She had so much to learn. She also needed to be restrained. He felt it clear to his bones that simply fucking her would give them both pleasure, but not compared to the heights they rose to when she was helpless to comply.

Chase rose to his knees and grabbed a wrist. "Would you feel better if I bound you?"

Her eyes grew wide. She didn't speak or move her head. Although the flare of her nose, the sharp intake of breath, and the heat in her eyes gave her away. He silently attached one wrist to the headboard with a leather cuff already connected by rope. He pulled the knot taut. Her arm was stretched so she couldn't move, but not so much she'd be in constant pain.

Out of nowhere Murphy appeared on the other side of the bed. He grabbed her other arm and repeated Chase's moves.

"More?"

"No, not this time." Chase settled back on the mattress, this time between the warmth of her legs.

Without a moment's hesitation, he slid two fingers through her slit. "You're very wet." He rimmed her swollen bud a few times before stroking from clit to anus. There he rubbed the tiny hole and watched Eve try to squirm away. "If this is what I want, will you say no?"

"I — I've never — "

"Why the hell not?" He left her backside and pushed his fingers deep inside her pussy. Her slick heat gripped him, forcing him deeper.

She struggled against her bonds, gasping for air.

"You're obviously open-minded and incredibly responsive to everything we've tried. How has no one taken you there?"

Still no answer…

He removed his fingers and lifted them to her mouth. "Open." He was starting to get annoyed by her lack of candor.

Eve shook her head.

With his other hand he tweaked a nipple, twisting until she cried out from the shock of pain. He pushed his fingers inside her mouth. Eve hesitantly stroked her tongue across his fingers, tasting herself. Chase's cock swelled at the sight and sensation of it, and Murphy groaned next to them.

"Aren't you going to join us?"

"Hell, no. This is too good of a show to miss." Murphy grasped his already hard cock in a tight fist and pumped.

Chase laughed and returned his attention to Eve. She'd begun to suck on his fingers like she'd done to his cock earlier. The pleasure was like an electric shot straight to his balls.

"I need a condom."

Murphy opened the bedside table and produced two. He threw one onto the bed and handed him the other. Chase cocked his eyebrow at the one lying on the sheets.

"What? I'm optimistic."

Chase shook his head and slid his fingers free from Eve. The slight moan of regret she made surprised him. Quickly he ripped into the condom and covered his cock. Eve's legs were spread wide, and the slight tremble he detected turned him on.

"She's so needy. Not sure if I should give in yet." Chase enjoyed the tease but knew damn well that waiting was out of the question. He placed the tip of his shaft at her slit and rubbed her up and down.

"Her pussy is practically begging you, Chase. Do it. Fuck her." Murphy pumped harder. The sounds of rough flesh on flesh filled the room.

Chase drove forward, taking her in one powerful thrust. Eve's head tipped back on a long cry, and Murphy moaned in tandem.

Holding still, Chase grabbed her bent legs and pushed them up her sides. In this position her pussy opened wide for deeper contact and she couldn't move her hips. He began an easy and controlled glide in and out, making sure to hit every nerve ending he could find.

"Chase—Oh God—Murphy!"

Chase laughed. "Well, which one is it?" He paused to wait for her answer.

"No, no, please don't stop."

Murphy crawled on the bed. Not close enough to touch, but enough to be clearly in her line of sight. Her eyes bugged wide at the vision of him jerking on his cock harder than she could imagine. She'd yet to experience the full extent of how rough he liked to get.

Chase leaned forward. "Imagine him fucking you like that, sweetheart. The heat and friction from a good hard fucking... You think you're ready for that?" His words taunted her, yet clearly did not dissuade her.

"Enough of that." He cupped her chin and brought her gaze to his. "Eyes on me. I'm the one fucking you."

He began slow, smooth strokes with his cock again, making sure to bump her sweet spot when their bodies met. Her clenching muscles did their level best to suck him deeper each and every time.

She looked him straight in the eye and said, "Harder. Please."

The throaty plea nearly stripped Chase of his control. Murphy's neck muscles flexed and bunched obscenely, evidencing his complete surrender to release. "Do it, Murph. Come on her."

Murphy pumped three times more and his cock erupted. Streams of cum covered her stomach and breasts. Eve fought furiously against her restraints, lost in a storm of sensation. With her eyes glazed and mouth open, she appeared totally immersed in enjoying the moment. She'd let go of whatever it was that kept holding her back.

Chase increased his pace, tunneling harder into Eve. Her body shook under the onslaught. Still she begged for more. Her need to come rode her hard, and he couldn't hold out any longer.

He pressed his finger against Eve's clit, the movement creating an involuntary rough jerk to spiral through her. Her whimpers turned to desperate cries. She was at the pinnacle of her release.

"Come, Eve. Come now."

Her eyes rolled back on a long wail. Her muscles gripped his dick so violently, the pleasure claimed his own release. The need for her was so strong that with cum pumping into the condom, fierce regret over not being able to come inside her tore him to shreds. The mere thought of skin-on-skin contact burned him alive.

Chase's arms and legs shook. His chest heaved as he fought for air. This woman rocked his world. Which wasn't something he admitted easily, even to himself. Watching her face go lax and her heavy breathing, he eased from her body. He averted his eyes from Murphy, who slowly moved from the bed. To meet his friend's gaze now would give away his vulnerability, and then he'd never fucking leave him alone.

Yes, he definitely needed to explore Eve and her submission. Without a doubt. But a long-term relationship between the three of them was simply out of the question. Chase removed the condom and dropped it into the bedside trash. He didn't want to leave her like this for long. He turned to make a beeline for the bathroom and came face-to-face with Murphy. Their gazes locked. The air between them thinned. Murphy studied him. Not exactly a hard task when he currently felt like an open book. Without a word he handed a warm, wet cloth to him and stood back — observing.

Chase returned to Eve's side and gently cleaned her. He easily removed the restraints from her wrists and rubbed them softly to ensure proper circulation. He recognized the soft, misty-eyed gaze she turned on him. They were on dangerous ground, and he should simply end things now and walk away. Job over. A good time had by all. But he couldn't — or wouldn't. What the hell was the difference at this point?

He pulled himself together and smiled down at her. She didn't know he ached for his camera right now. That the desire to capture her afterglow ate away at his resolve.

"I bet you'd enjoy a hot shower right about now." Murphy leaned across the mattress and planted a kiss on Eve's hip.

A slow smile spread across her face, followed by a slight blush. "I need to go home. It must be getting late by now." She began to move from the bed, and Chase captured her legs.

"Uh-uh. Not so fast."

"Are we not done with the photos?" The worried look on her face almost made him laugh. Their scared little sub was ready to rabbit out of the building.

"We've got more than we need for the client." He trailed his fingers from the inside of her ankle to the back of her knee, her stiff inhale a reward that spurred him on. "I have a new proposal for you."

Eve struggled to sit up. He held her firmly in place. "At least let me cover myself." She crossed her arms over her breasts and frowned, marring her forehead with worry lines.

"No," both men said in unison.

"We like you just like this. In fact I'd like to see a lot more of you like this."

"What—What are you saying?"

Chase couldn't quite name the emotion he saw in her gaze. Not quite fear. Not quite happiness. Wariness maybe.

"I'd like to take more pictures."

"But I thought you said you had enough."

"Yes, for the client. These would not be for anyone but myself."

"And me," Murphy chimed in.

NINE

Blood rushed to Eve's head as she struggled and scrambled against Chase's hold. When he didn't immediately release her, panic began to set in.

"Let me up, Chase. Please." Her heart raced and sweat popped out across her brow. Seconds ticked by with nothing from Chase but his intense glare. That gaze bore into her as if he could see straight through her. Past the fear to the dark and secret fantasies she still harbored. A relationship she dared not speak out loud.

"Maybe we should step back. Get some food. We all missed lunch."

Eve glanced gratefully at Murphy. She needed a few minutes more to get her wits about her. First clothes, then food. She had a crazy need to be on equal footing with them before she continued this conversation.

Chase lifted himself from the bed and released her legs. "Sure. Sounds like a plan to me." The heat of his gaze did not match the casual tone of his words.

"How about I order some takeout from next door and we eat in your office." Murphy paused, waiting for Chase's response.

"Yeah, fine." He shoved his legs into the pants he'd discarded on the floor. "I'm anxious to start uploading the new shots anyways." He gave her one long last glance, the barely banked heat clearly visible in his gaze. "I'll meet y'all in there."

With that, he strode from the room, leaving Murphy and her alone. She wrapped the loose silk sheet nice and tight around her body. "He has a horrible habit of doing that."

"What's that?"

"Walking away." His need to have the last word as he walked from a room often left her scrambling between needing to cry and wanting to laugh.

"There isn't much he doesn't want to be in charge of. Including conversations. Left to his own devices, he'd have pushed a hell of a lot harder." Murphy walked over to the wardrobe and hung the suit he'd worn for the shoot inside. Mesmerized once again by his incredible body and the movement of his tattoo when his muscles flexed, Eve sat down on her heels and watched him get dressed.

"I'm beginning to think you are quite the little voyeur."

If he only knew.

She covered her mouth to hide her grin. There was no denying she'd happily crawl to him just for the chance to bite his ass.

"Is it improper for me to stare?" she chided.

Murphy crossed back to the bed, jeans still unfastened and shirt wide open to the lickable muscles of his chest. He cupped her chin and tilted her head back, forcing her eyes to meet his. "If we were still in scene, I'd drag you across my knee for disrespect."

Eve swallowed past the lump in her throat, doing the best she could to ignore the flutter of excitement that coursed through her. She'd just had more orgasms than she thought possible, yet he still aroused her intensely. She had an acute desire to know what a spanking from Murphy would feel like. It took every ounce of her control not to moan at the image of him warming her ass with his hands.

"You're killing me."

"What?" she whispered, her voice more breathless than she'd expected.

"You think I can't see what you're thinking. Babe, it's clear as day in those pretty eyes of yours. Unfortunately, I suggested dinner, and we need to talk."

Eve screwed up her face in disappointment. Even if he was right. She did not need to get swept up in the things these two men made her feel. Chase had made an unexpected suggestion, and she'd need her wits about her to figure out what the hell he was up to.

"Get dressed and meet me in Chase's office. I should be able to get dinner quickly."

He released her face, and she dropped her chin to hide her disappointment. How he got to her so easily amazed her. Or maybe it was simply the fact it had been so damn long since she'd been in any kind of relationship.

Even a sexual one.

And she had no doubt Chase and Murphy wanted nothing more than to live out a few fantasies, have a good time, get some great pictures, and then move on. When the door closed behind Murphy, the noise roused her from her thoughts. She leaped from the bed to scavenge her clothing. Focused on her task, she almost missed the mirror directly in front of her.

Her appearance froze her in place. The woman staring back at her barely resembled the woman she'd been at six a.m. this morning when she'd paced her bedroom, deciding on the perfect outfit.

The makeup was gone, the hair went every which way, and the marks scattered across her body were all signs of a well-used woman. A serene warmth spread from her belly to every region of her body. For the first time in quite a while, she saw what they saw in the mirror — a sexual woman capable of many sexual and loving things. Not just a caregiver to her sick family. Or the landlady of a crumbling building.

Here, with Chase and Murphy, she'd been transformed into so much more. It gave her hope for the future no matter where it led her. If they wanted to spend more time with her and teach her about the lifestyle they loved, as well as delve into her fantasies a little deeper, she'd say yes. Her brain told her it was the worst mistake she could make, getting attached to these two men. But her body screamed *hell yeah*, and the need they'd unfurled wasn't ready to be tucked away quite yet.

Eve scooped her clothes from the floor and began to get dressed. She'd have liked to admire the marks they'd left on her body a bit longer, but there'd be time for that tonight when she went home. She feared once she was alone again the events of the day would come crashing down. Eventually she'd have to deal with the small twinge of guilt making her feel uncomfortable.

Two men. God, she wasn't a fucking prude by any stretch of the imagination, and a ménage with Chase and Murphy had starred in many a secret fantasy when she took the time to indulge in getting herself off, but now it wasn't just a dream any longer. She'd actually done it. Did that make her a deviant now? Or worse?

Eve fastened the last of the buttons and swiped her hand through her messy hair. She leaned into the mirror and looked closer. What kind of woman took two men to bed? Apparently her kind.

She fought the mess her hair had become, tamping down the guilt. She had nothing to feel bad about. They were all consenting adults with specific needs. Just because she wanted to be restrained so badly she ached didn't make her a freak.

Surprisingly she enjoyed working here. It had become a fun place to escape to as well as make the money she desperately needed to keep things afloat.

"You're stalling." She spoke to herself in the mirror. She'd indulged in her own thoughts long enough. Chase and Murphy had a proposal for her, and above the layer of fear of getting too close, lay the hope that the more she experienced, the more she'd be able to cope on her own in the future.

Eve straightened her spine and thrust out her breasts in a show of defiance. She could definitely do this. On that positive thought, she strode from the room with only a brief wistful glance at the bed she'd just shared with Chase and Murphy.

God help her if she was making a huge mistake and walking into something she couldn't handle.

* * *

Eve stood in the doorway and studied Chase. With his head bent over the computer screen, she couldn't tell what he was looking at, but she guessed it would be the photos he'd just taken. At least he'd said he was anxious to look at them.

As usual his thick brown hair seemed to go in every direction. Whenever he was stressed or even simply thinking hard about something, he'd tunnel those strong fingers of his through the strands and generally make a mess. It served as the only true way to be sure he was getting carried away with his work. The man had the clear and calm look on his face so down pat he could fool just about anyone.

With one hand he worked the mouse, and with the other he scribbled notes on a piece of paper. She'd always thought him being left-handed made his work like this a lot easier. He clicked through pictures so fast she barely caught flashes of red as he went through them. She guessed he was looking at the pictures of her on the bed.

Loath to interrupt, she waited as long as she could stand it. But the need to see the pictures called out to her as well. She'd never been particularly fond of getting her photo taken, but somehow she'd known Chase would capture something entirely different. And if what they kept stating was true and they truly liked her body the way it was, flaws and all, she trusted Chase had once again captured her perfectly.

"Did they turn out okay?"

Chase minimized whatever he'd been working on and slowly swiveled in his chair. The look in his eyes took her breath away. The hard planes of his face stood out strong, and his lips were compressed in a near frown, but if the eyes were the window to the soul, then Chase was the big bad wolf and he wanted to eat her.

"They are perfect." He pushed back from the desk and stood. Immediately Eve's gaze was drawn to the bulge straining at his crotch. Heat suffused her face at the fact her pictures had turned him on. This was very cool indeed. "Come here. I'll show you."

He held out his hand for her, and she moved forward. The second she placed her hand in his, he jerked her forward and into his arms. Eve lost her balance, but Chase caught her effortlessly. Crushed against the heat of his chest, she had the overwhelming urge to burrow in.

She breathed deeply, hoping to calm her racing heart, and instead got a noseful of his decadent scent. The rich musk of sex with a subtle hint of pine soap underneath. Eve rubbed against him. The hard ridge of his erection pressed against her served as the perfect reminder of how much he wanted her.

Her pussy clenched for more. Sore muscles be damned, she ached for him to take what he needed. In fact, the image of him bending her over the desk, flipping up her skirt, and fucking her mercilessly from behind would have brought her to her knees had he not been hanging on to her.

"Eve, look at me."

She tilted her head back and met his gaze. Molten heat met ferocious need. Her pussy squeezed in response. Everything from the way he held her to the fierce look in his eyes spoke to something deep inside her. The part better left alone. She knew now there would be no escaping without a broken heart. She only hoped there'd be enough of her left to put the pieces back together.

Chase leaned forward and pressed his lips to hers. A small groan sounded at the back of her throat as roaring heat raced into her. With his tongue, he traced the soft skin of her mouth, and she eagerly opened to his exploration. But it was when he slid his hand into her hair and grabbed a fistful and pulled just to the point of tiny tingles racing along her scalp that did her in.

He shifted his long body against hers until his knee pressed between her thighs. Moments later he pushed against her covered mound, the pressure barely glancing across her clit. Fire raged through Eve from Chase's touch. The man had a way of teasing her that drove her insane. Her nipples ached with every brush of fabric, and it wasn't long before she wanted to come again.

He bit down on her bottom lip, sending fresh jolts of pain and pleasure to every erogenous zone on her body. Eve gasped, grasping his biceps in a tight grip.

Chase jerked away from her. "No, don't touch me. I don't have enough control for that right now, and trust me, darling, you aren't ready for what I'm feeling right now."

Disappointed, Eve allowed her arms to slide down her body, away from the contact she desperately needed. She pursed her lips and didn't even bother to hide the longing she felt.

"Don't look like that or I'll start to believe you're an insatiable minx."

"Who's an insatiable minx? Eve?" Murphy strode into the office carrying an armful of bags from the Chinese restaurant next door.

"Saved this time. But don't think I'm going to forget about that pout. I think a nice red ass would clear that right up," Chase whispered in her ear.

"I was about to show Eve some of the shots from today." Chase quickly sat in his chair and pulled her down onto his lap.

"Masterpieces, I'm sure." Murphy settled the bags on the coffee table and moved in behind Chase's chair. "Let's see 'em."

Chase swiveled the chair to face the monitor and clicked the mouse to enlarge the image he'd hidden earlier. An oversize, up-close shot of her naked and bound on red silk sheets filled the screen. A low whistle from Murphy sounded near her ear.

"Gorgeous."

Murphy's compliment warmed her insides, even though it was clearly Chase's talent in capturing a subject at the perfect angle and all the other factors he considered that made her look so good. And yes, even she thought she looked good. She imagined having this photo hung at the foot of her bed. Something for her to look back on and remember after this was all over.

"What do you think, beautiful?"

"I think you are the most talented photographer in the world. I don't know how you did it, but you made me look so…"

"Submissive."

Chase murmured his agreement. Eve swore the air in the room thickened and tension seeped from both men. Not to mention the erection poking her in the butt seemed to keep growing.

She moved the word submissive around in her head, trying to come to terms with it. She'd never thought to apply that word to herself. In everything she'd studied, she'd preferred to simply label herself kinky.

Chase scrolled through a few other pictures, which she barely noticed. She was still back on what they'd called her. It didn't seem to work, yet when she looked at the photographic evidence, she couldn't deny that she looked different.

Peaceful.

When was the last time she'd applied that word to her life? Maybe never. Even before her parents got sick, they drove her mad with their selfish ways. Eve squeezed her eyes shut and fought back the tears suddenly threatening to fall. How could she think of her dead mother like that?

She'd never understood what kept them together to the very end though. Her father had been absorbed in his life. His work, his hobbies, and his mistresses.

Eve struggled in Chase's lap. She needed to get out of here before she started to fall apart.

"Stop."

Eve stilled at the firm command. Stuck between a rock and a hard place, she held her breath and counted to five before exhaling a long, slow breath.

"You're shaking. What's wrong?" Chase wrapped himself around her and spun the chair around so she had to face Murphy.

"Nothing. I—I—"

"If you tell me you're fine, I will turn you over my knee and paddle your ass until you can't sit down for days."

Eve blinked at the pressure in her eyes, but nothing helped. Murphy pulled her from Chase's lap and into his arms, where she burst into tears.

TEN

Murphy knew the second she would lose it. What had triggered the outburst, he had no idea. He carried her to the couch and sat down. With her cradled against his chest, he waited out the tears. Chase gave him a questioning look, and he shrugged. What could he say? It was possible she hadn't fully recovered from the scene and seeing the pictures had brought a flood of emotion crashing down on her.

Eve shuddered violently in his arms with full-blown racking sobs. Whatever she'd held pent up inside had desperately needed to come out. Now they just needed to find out what it was.

He brushed his hand across the top of her head and placed a kiss at her ear. "Let it all out, Eve. I've got you."

And the sudden realization that he didn't want to let her go hit him like a sucker punch to the solar plexus. But did he know her well enough to keep her?

He'd been so certain before, and look how great that had turned out. Eve wasn't like *her* though. She wasn't sophisticated and manipulative. In fact, he'd never met a more down-to-earth woman in his life. Everything about her screamed practical, except for the damned shoes. She had been torturing him for months with her goddamned fuck-me shoes. Dozens of them. He wondered if she even realized that four-inch heels put her at the perfect height to be bent over a desk and fucked from behind.

He did. And he'd had the hard-ons to prove it.

Of course now he also knew she had more secrets than why she wore sexy heels and incredible lingerie. They'd touched on something deeper, and now he had to know what.

Several long minutes later her sobs had decreased to sniffles, and he pointed to the box of tissues on the cabinet behind Chase. His friend grabbed it and came around the desk. When Chase settled on the couch next to him and placed a hand at the small of her back, Murphy had to bite back a satisfied smile.

The bastard wasn't as cold as he wanted everyone to believe. The destruction left behind in the wake of their previous relationship had affected him, and everything leading to tonight had colored his behavior. Murphy's inclination was to push Chase. To force him to see what Eve could be to them, but deep down he knew he'd have to wait him out. Forcing Chase to do anything was out of the question.

Murphy passed a tissue to Eve and waited for her to pull herself together. She needed to be calm before they questioned her. Instinct told him she'd try to run—an option neither he nor Chase would allow.

Long moments passed where the only sound came from the last of Eve's sniffles and the hum of Chase's computer. For Murphy, fatigue had begun to set in. With his head resting against the back of the leather sofa, it would be easy enough to fall asleep where he sat. Eve had quit squirming, and her breathing had settled into a steady rhythm. He suspected she'd fully recovered and was now afraid or embarrassed to make a move.

When her stomach rumbled, he lifted her from his chest and stared into her red-rimmed eyes. "You're hungry."

She nodded.

The seat cushion shifted, and Chase moved toward the bags of food. He removed container after container along with the plates and silverware Murphy had requested from the restaurant. He'd wanted Eve to know he had more style than to make her eat out of containers.

Ideally he would have bundled her into his car and taken her to their condo. That image made him smile. She was far too skittish at the moment to be dragged off for more kinky adventures. He'd at least give her a minute or two.

"What's so funny?"

"I was thinking about what I wanted to do with you."

Her face perked up. "Do I even want to know?"

"Probably not yet. Turn around and get some food. We have time for that later."

She stared back at him for a few more minutes. Probably trying to figure out what he was up to. Eventually she scooted from his lap and took a spot between Chase and him on the couch.

"What kind of Chinese do you like? I pretty much got a little of everything."

"Any orange chicken?"

"Ahh, a woman after my own heart." Chase spoke up and handed her the extra-large container he'd been holding.

"It's his favorite."

"Oohh, mine too. This and a little fried rice and I'm in heaven." She scooped food onto her plate and settled back in her seat. Murphy glanced at Chase over her head and nodded his assent.

"Eve, why do you live in that building?"

Eve froze, fork halfway to her mouth.

Curious, Murphy watched her body language carefully. One of the first things he'd learned when he entered the scene was the importance of body language. All the hype given about safe words and shit was exactly that. Hype. Often a submissive became too far gone in a scene to utter the safe word, or too damned stubborn.

He'd met many a bratty and willful sub more determined to impress him with how far she'd be willing to go, rather than actually taking the time to really get to know him so they'd both benefit. It depressed him how many women couldn't wrap their heads around the fact that their pleasure was his pleasure, and it was his duty and right to give it when he deemed it appropriate.

It had been that guiding principle that had led Chase and him not only into the scene, but in the search for a submissive to share.

Eve stared into her food. She'd stopped eating, and based on the way she fidgeted with the fork, he'd guess she was lost in some sort of memory. Longing to touch her, he reached out and stroked her hair. The soft strands caressed his fingers. His cock tightened and strained against his pants. It seemed no matter what they did, she aroused him.

"The building belongs to my stepfather." Her answer came out on a hoarse croak. "When he got sick, it kinda became my responsibility."

Ah… Now they were getting somewhere.

"Is he…" Murphy hated to ask the question.

Eve shook her head furiously. "Oh no, he's still alive and for the most part well. About six months ago I moved him into a local assisted-living facility. He has Alzheimer's."

Chase and he both nodded. She'd spoken the words calmly enough, although the frown lines on her forehead made him curious. There was definitely more to her story.

Presuming they were satisfied, she returned to her meal and they all finished in silence. When all the food and drink had been consumed and Chase's office restored to order, Murphy pulled Eve between them.

"You certainly don't offer much detail about yourself, do you?"

She blinked up at him. "I didn't think it mattered here. I do my job, whatever that may be, then I go home to my personal life and trudge through that."

"See, that's exactly what I'm talking about. Why are you trudging along? Honestly, Eve, that doesn't sound fun at all." Murphy reached for another lock of her hair and twirled it between his fingers. He needed to stop thinking about sex, but he couldn't stop touching her.

"Today was the most fun I've had in a long time," she whispered.

"Why? What's been holding you back?" Chase asked.

A deep sigh sounded from Eve, compressing her tighter in his arms.

"You aren't going to let this go, are you?"

"No." They answered in unison.

Eve pushed and wiggled from their embrace. She moved away from them, and this time they let her go. "A few years ago, my mother got sick. Cancer."

Murphy's heart sank at the gravelly, pain-filled sound of her voice.

"My stepfather's dementia was still in its early stages, but he refused to help her. He claimed his work required more of his attention, and since he was the sole breadwinner in the family, I moved in to help my mom."

"Nice guy." Murphy couldn't resist the jab. Assholes like him were everywhere.

"You don't know the half of it." Her hands twisted together in her lap. Likely a subconscious move.

"Why don't you tell us," Chase interjected.

"Suffice it to say, my stepdad would definitely not win any awards for parenting or being a husband. My mom was everything that held the family together, and her death changed everything."

"Changed how?" Murphy had to work at not pulling her into his arms. Eve was a proud woman, and he sensed she needed the little bit of distance at the moment.

"I'd always planned to strike out on my own, find my way in the world, and no sooner did I get out, I was pulled back in again. So when my mom's cancer took a turn for the worse, I started making plans for the future." She jumped up from the sofa and strode across the room and back again.

"And?" Chase sounded as impatient as he felt.

"Her last wish was that I take care of Jim. That's my stepdad. By the time of her death, his Alzheimer's had progressed to the point he needed a lot more help than I could give. So she made me promise not to leave him, to ensure he was well taken care of."

"So that's why you live in the building. You're taking care of it for him."

"Yes."

"That's an awful lot of responsibility you've been carrying around for a while."

She came within reach on her latest pass of the room, and Murphy jerked her onto his lap. Eve squeaked when she fell. He dropped a kiss on her forehead. Then frowned.

"Where does the money for this building come from? Did your stepfather set up a trust for you before his health declined?"

Eve dug her teeth into her bottom lip. "No, he refused to trust me with his money. He was convinced I couldn't handle it. Even now on his rare lucid occasions he complains. Now all the money goes to his care."

"Hence your job here, then." Chase touched her cheek, and she leaned into his hand.

She was drowning in a sea of responsibility and had chosen them to share her pain. By trusting in them enough to act out her fantasies and needs.

"This half life you've been living isn't much of a life at all. Certainly not the one you need." Chase tangled his fingers in her hair and tugged her head back until their gazes met.

"Why did you start crying?" Chase questioned her.

Murphy watched the play-by-play between them. The heat they exchanged without even realizing it.

"Tell me."

"You called me submissive."

The expression on Chase's face changed. Nothing overtly obvious, but to someone who'd known him for twenty years it was obvious. The slight flattening of his lips, the shuttered lids, and even the slight flare of his nose.

"You don't like being called a sub?"

"Chase, I don't think I'm truly submissive. Yes, I have a lot of kinky fantasies and being tied up gives me a sense of freedom I can't get any other way, but I like to be in control of my own life. Not following someone else's will. I've done enough of that in my life."

"And it's just that simple?"

"Nothing is ever simple. It's the lesson I keep learning over and over." The bitterness of that statement filled the room. Something Murphy wanted to take from her.

She squeezed her eyes closed, and Murphy took that moment to rub her thigh. She jerked under his hand. He continued. He liked the idea she was fighting her nature and she needed to get used to his touch. He'd love the opportunity to prove her wrong.

Chase's hand tightened on her nape as he moved closer, his lips hovering near her ear.

"You fight too much, little one. It's time for you to do something for yourself for a change."

"We...uh...I did. I posed for pictures and you and...uh...Murphy..."

"Yes, you did. Was it enough? Are you ready to simply go back to the way things were?"

Murphy traced her thigh to the heat between her legs. Already her panties were damp. He brushed across her mound, and she jerked in his lap. Her lids lifted, and the naked heat in her eyes did him in.

ELEVEN

The woman was as willful as they came. Chase bit at her earlobe while Murphy pulled the panties from under her skirt. Little did she know she'd let them in enough for them to figure out exactly what she needed and how far she'd go without getting broken.

This wasn't how he'd planned to put his proposal to her, but he was nothing if not flexible. This kind of thing was expected with an untrained submissive. The depth to which she wanted to go wasn't completely clear as of yet, and testing her would be a hell of a lot of fun for them all.

"This doesn't have to be the end yet. We've barely scratched the surface."

Murphy slid a finger through the folds of her pussy, and the resulting moan from Eve sent a kick to his self-control, reminding him that this woman had more power than she realized. He'd need to tread carefully.

"You really do make the perfect model for me. You are like a lovely lush piece of fruit begging for someone to pluck you from the vine."

"Is that a nice way to say I'm a desperate fat girl?"

Thwack!

Eve screeched at the abrupt slap across her inner thigh. Chase smiled at Murphy's quick thinking.

"You don't want to disrespect us like that again. Do not piss me off, Eve."

"I'm sorry, I was only kidding."

"Anything that involves you degrading something I covet or own is not very amusing. I expect I won't hear something like that come out of your mouth again."

"Yes." She nodded.

"Yes, what?" Chase knew she'd know what he meant, and now seemed as good a time as any to start reinforcing it. She had no idea how badly he wanted to discipline her for her ridiculous comment.

"Yes, Sir." He recognized the obvious hesitation and let it go for now. They had plenty of time to keep working on protocols.

"Now as I was saying. The photographs I've taken so far represent some of my best work. I've had a project in mind for a long time, and this is the first time I've come across a model who fits what I'm looking for."

"But as you pointed out, I'm not a model."

Chase shook his head. If she wasn't careful, she'd be going from the willful category and straight into bratty. And bratty subs did not enjoy his brand of punishment.

"The fact you're not a professional model is what has made you the perfect subject in this case. Despite your insistence that you aren't submissive, your expressions and movements and even actions speak a totally different story."

"But—"

Chase covered her mouth with his hand. "Just listen, beautiful. Stop fighting."

While they'd been talking, Murphy had rubbed the spot he'd smacked, where a perfect red streak had appeared. He'd noticed more than once Eve widening her legs and giving Murphy better access to her cunt.

"You have fantasies. I dare to guess deep, dark ones you've never shared with anyone. Am I right?"

"Yes."

"We can help you with those. Give you a safe haven for exploration."

"And you want to capture that on film?"

"Yes, I do."

"That sounds kind of... I don't know. Disconnected." Her upper body shuddered on the last word. Murphy had gone back to finger fucking her, and his wicked hands were starting to get to her.

"Taking pictures is what I do, Eve. It is how I show the world what I see. It would be an honor to capture your expressions as you experience them."

Chase bit down on the shell of her ear just hard enough to give her a quick thrill of pain to add to Murphy's movements.

"What would I have to do?"

"Anything and everything I command. You'd be ours to do with as we please. If you want a safe word, I'll give you one. Although I'd caution you to use it wisely. Our intent will be to push your boundaries. To test you beyond your normal limits. There is a lot to explore, and everything I've seen so far makes me believe you need this too."

Chase swallowed past the lump forming in his throat. The perfume of her sex filled the room, and the thick wave of lust pushed at his patience.

Eve shivered against him.

"What questions do you have?"

"I'm nervous." Her tongue darted out to lick her lips. His cock throbbed at the sight. Damn, he wanted to take her mouth. Watch her mouth stretch wide as she worked to make him fit. Not the time. Chase steeled himself against his stray thoughts.

Chase licked across the lobe of her ear. "I'd be worried if you weren't a little afraid. Try to relax. Let us help you." He bit his way along her jawline until he was inches away from their mouths touching, their breath mingled.

"Come, Eve, come now."

Her eyes grew wide and her pert mouth opened to scream, but no sound came out. Her body shuddered and jerked against him, every muscle spasming with her release.

Murphy moaned and moved to lap at her slit. When Eve would have jackknifed forward from the extreme pleasure, Chase held her down and made her ride it out while restrained. As much as he wanted to fuck her again, he'd make himself wait until tomorrow night. The buildup from need and anticipation would serve his purposes well.

Spent, Eve collapsed against his chest. Murphy dislodged his fingers and smiled wickedly when he brought three soaking-wet fingers to his mouth. Oh yes, their little submissive wouldn't live in denial much longer.

Chase brushed the wet hair from her face and lifted her gently. "Murphy is going to take you home tonight. Tomorrow is Saturday and I expect you to get some rest. Drink lots of fluids as well. At midnight, we will pick you up. You can wear whatever you like because you won't need it for long. Until then, everything else will be a surprise."

Chase turned her at an angle and cupped her cheek. "Do you understand my instructions?"

"I can't help but think—"

He gripped her tighter. "That's your problem right now. You think too much when all you really need to do is obey. Trust us to take care of you."

Eve nodded.

"Good, now turn around and give me a proper kiss good-bye."

TWELVE

Eve rushed around her apartment cleaning up the mess she'd made trying to get ready. She'd indulged in every girly ritual she could think of to keep her mind off the nerves. Of course none of that worked. But at least she looked good. She'd fluffed, colored, primped, and even removed every strand of hair from her private parts. That had been the coolest part. Without hair covering her skin, everything seemed more sensitive.

She hadn't thought to ask if they would mind, but considering every single model she'd ever witnessed had no body hair, she suspected it was one of those expected things.

Since they'd given her complete freedom to wear what she wanted, she'd opted for a simple summer dress. It was light and airy and left her completely accessible. She'd given so much thought to every word Chase had spoken and still couldn't quite reconcile what they wanted with what she wanted. Sure the sexual aspect of it thrilled her, but anything beyond that seemed frightening — restrictive.

Fortunately, Chase had not mentioned anything beyond another photo project, so she'd taken him at his word and talked herself down every time her mind wandered to something bigger. Looking for anything more was the sure path to a broken heart. Something she'd had enough of.

The knock on the door announced their arrival. Eve threw the last of her rejected clothing into the closet and slammed the door. Just so long as no one looked in there, nothing would be out of place.

Eve yanked open the door and grinned at the sight of Murphy and Chase lingering in her doorway. Both men wore snug jeans that rode low on their hips, but that was where the similarities stopped. Chase had chosen a black T-shirt that did little to hide the defined muscles she now knew resided under his shirt. Murphy, on the other hand, had gone with a royal blue button-down. Already her fingers itched to help him out of it. Eve knew this was the moment to sink or swim. Go for it and deal with the broken heart later when it was over, or back out and always wonder what could have been.

She already knew she was going for it.

They continued to stare at each other for long, charged moments before Eve spoke. "Would you like to come in?" She stepped back and waited for them to enter.

They walked in, filling the space around her. Murphy cupped her chin and brought his lips to hers for a quick kiss. "Nice place. Did you do all this yourself?" He motioned around her apartment.

"Yes, it's pretty much the only way I could stand to stay here. Surrounding myself with pretty things helped a lot."

"You don't like it here?"

"I like the building. It has good bones." Luckily they didn't press her further.

Chase and Murphy both nodded. "Are you ready to go?"

"Where are we going?" She wasn't sure what they were up to since she'd thought they would stay here.

"Now what would be the fun in telling you in advance?" Murphy shot her a wicked grin.

Both men crowded around her. Chase in the front and Murphy in the back. With them this close in proximity, her nipples tightened and the brush of fabric across them made her gasp.

"I brought something for you to wear." Chase handed her a black blindfold. The silk cloth fell into her hand, caressing the skin with cool fabric.

"Hold it up over your eyes, sweetheart," Murphy whispered from behind her. "I'll tie it for you."

Eve did as she was instructed and covered her eyes. The nervous butterflies fluttered in her stomach again, which did nothing to curb the wetness covering the bare folds of her pussy.

"Are you claustrophobic or anything?" Chase asked.

"No. I'm fine."

Murphy's hands traveled down her back and cupped her ass through the flimsy material of her dress. Eve couldn't believe how much she already ached with need. When he slipped under her hemline, she spread her legs and allowed him full access.

He slid his hand through the crevice of her ass, a single finger sliding over her tiny hole. Heat shot through her from the tip of her head all the way to the tips of her toes. She'd fantasized about this all day long. It was the ultimate thing for her. The one dark longing she'd never been able to get out of her head after all these years. She wanted both men at the same time, filling her pussy and ass.

Before she even realized what she was doing, Eve arched forward, pressing her body into Chase. She gasped at the shocks of pleasure created from the slight friction.

"I take it you haven't changed your mind," Chase murmured, his breath hot across her cheek.

Eve looked down between their bodies and fervently wished they were both naked. She needed nothing more than hot skin against hot skin. These men made her want everything she'd ever denied herself and more. Hell, she didn't even know what all she wanted. The answer was simply Chase and Murphy. She desperately hoped she could give them everything they desired.

Chase reached for the nipples she arched in his direction. In response to her wanton ways, he pinched and twisted them both. A sharp mix of pain and pleasure infused her, and she cried out.

"We're going to go deep, Eve. Murphy and I will discover each and every one of your fantasies. You will beg. Possibly for more. Probably to make it stop. But you will feel like never before."

Deep-seated need jolted her body. With Chase manipulating her nipples and Murphy stroking her backside, she knew where this was headed, and despite any residual fear, she couldn't wait to get there.

Chase dropped his hands and took a step away from her. Murphy quickly followed.

"Let's go." Chase nodded toward the door.

Murphy scooped her into his arms, where she wrapped her hands around his neck. "Might as well carry you rather than try to direct you. Much easier."

For a split second she worried he would find her heavy and difficult to carry. She opened her mouth to say so when she remembered what they'd said before. Wisely, she chose to keep her mouth shut this time. If he decided he didn't want to keep her in his arms, he could simply put her down and lead her out. Besides, she had much better things to focus on.

Still reeling from the heightened state of her arousal, Eve left the safety of her apartment and headed into the unknown with Chase and Murphy.

* * *

Chase followed Murphy and Eve down the stairs. More than once he'd reached down to adjust the front of his jeans. His hard cock dug into the metal teeth of the zipper until he thought it would bust open. He concentrated on the slight bite of pain. Maybe it would help him get his mind focused on the plan for tonight, versus the need to bend her over the hood of his car and drive into her over and over again.

Something about this woman brought out the baser side of his nature. How many times would he have to fuck her until he got it out of his system? Ten? Twenty?

At the car, he slid into the driver's seat and let Murphy get in the back with Eve. He needed to keep some distance between them for now. The shoot he'd planned for tonight had the makings of his best ever, and he didn't want to fuck it up. As much as he wanted to sink into her soft, feminine flesh, he'd get the job done first.

In the small confines of his car, her fresh, clean scent filled the air. A simple fragrance that tugged at his resistance. He didn't have to turn around to imagine her naked form tied in rope. Her high breasts with their responsive tips were foremost in his mind. Every move they'd made over the last few days made her wetter than the last. The photo shoot for the client had been a walk in the park compared to what he had in mind. Chase laughed at his own pun.

He'd paid a lot of money for the permit for tonight's use of a public playground. Somehow he knew it would be worth every damned penny. She had the body of a pinup and the mind of a strong-willed submissive. The person or persons who managed to tame her would be well rewarded. Now he just had to find his way inside the last of her armor and get her to surrender completely.

Tonight they'd discover her limits. She had no idea of the controls he had in place. So the fear he photographed would be genuine. As would the need. The distinct scent of leather and the sound of buckles being fastened filled his senses. Excitement coursed through Chase's veins as he glanced in the rearview mirror. His delicious Eve sat on Murphy's lap while he fastened her new wrist cuffs.

No one spoke, but the tension between them ratcheted to an all-new level. So far she'd managed to stay calm and agreeable through what they demanded. Now he wondered how much she would fight them. When they had her shackled and helpless, she'd be more vulnerable than she'd ever been.

They'd learned a lot about her life last night, and it had given him information he needed to create tonight's scene. She was a strong and proud woman who'd worked her ass off in the face of hard times.

How many years had passed since someone had seen to her pleasure? Her eagerness to explore and accept what they'd asked told him more than her words ever could. Caring for aging and sick parents took a lot of work, and the fact it hadn't dampened her spirit impressed him. She'd found a small happiness in surrounding herself with beautiful things to brighten a situation that could have taken down a lesser woman.

Patience and perseverance would be his best tools when dealing with her. Although tonight he'd make it more about pushing and demanding more than anyone ever had. Her fear of the word submissive concerned him. If he couldn't get to her on a mental level, they'd never be successful.

He wanted to get to the fantasies she'd harbored all this time. She deserved someone who took the time to savor her, to unpeel the layers and give her the freedom to act out on every sexual desire she'd ever considered. Nothing would be too wicked for Eve.

Chase pulled into the empty parking lot and stopped close to the gate. The headlights from his car highlighted the mist from the lake clinging to the ground. The weather and humidity levels were practically tailor-made tonight. He stepped from the car and breathed in the warm night air. Excitement inside him built. He was anxious to get started.

He strode to the trunk and opened it. He'd planned to haul in his gear before they let Eve out of the car. Murphy and he had discussed the stress she would experience once she realized they were shooting outside, so they would restrain her together. A sort of shock-and-awe treatment.

The spot he'd chosen wasn't far from the car, so he had everything carried over and set up in less than fifteen minutes. Every muscle pulled taut while he worked, and it had nothing to do with strenuous labor. He'd set the lighting for a shoot a million times. No, it was the woman he was dying to get his hands on and the scene he'd prepared for her.

This part of the anticipation was almost as exciting as the torment he'd soon put her through.

The careful planning so he and Murphy could control the scene at all times. There'd be no point in asking for her trust if they couldn't keep her safe.

The playground was part of a secluded county park on private property that closed at dusk. During the day, the place was packed with boaters and families enjoying the outdoors. Tonight not a soul could be found for miles. The lone security guard wouldn't come near this area for hours. Not that Eve would know that.

Chase checked over all of his gear one last time to ensure all the settings were correct before heading back to the car.

As he approached the rear door, he noticed Murphy's hand between Eve's lush thighs. He'd known his friend wouldn't keep his hands off her, and he didn't blame him a bit. He knew the deal not to give her the release she'd beg for.

That would come much later.

Eve whimpered at the third finger Murphy sank into her drenched pussy. He'd been working her for what seemed like forever, and she was on the verge of an out-of-this-world explosion. Her legs shook.

"Oh...Murphy... Please." She didn't care for a second about the fact she begged. She'd been strung tight since they'd knocked on her door, and all that mattered now was the release she ached for. How easily they got her to focus solely on what they did to her.

"No, Eve. Not yet. If you come now, then not only will you be punished, but you'll mess up his photo shoot."

"Then—" She could barely breathe, let alone speak. "Stop."

Murphy growled into the soft curve of her neck. "No."

Eve tossed her head from side to side on his chest, trying to wiggle from his grasp. He only shoved inside her farther. "I can't—"

"You can and you will," he insisted.

Suddenly the door on her left side opened and a cool rush of night air swept through the car. Her nipples tightened into points hard as ice. Eve cried out. Not from fear. No, her nipples and pretty much every other inch of bared skin had grown intensely sensitive.

"Murphy, please."

Immediately, he withdrew his fingers from her sex and left her empty and unfulfilled.

"We've already had this talk."

Eve pushed through the fog in her brain, trying to figure out where she'd gone wrong. It took her a few seconds, but she eventually processed it.

"I'm sorry, Sir."

Chase chuckled from the vicinity of the open door. "I see that's going to take some practice. Or at the very least a little discipline."

Murphy brushed her dress back down, covering her breasts and leaving the fabric to pool at her hips. "C'mon, beautiful, we have a big night ahead of us."

"Reach for me, Eve." Chase spoke.

Blindly she reached her arms in the direction of his voice, and he grabbed her hands. She scooted to the edge of the bench seat, and Chase helped her step from the car.

"I don't suppose you plan to tell me where we are?"

"Nope. But we're almost there. I'll take care of you." Chase's voice warmed her insides. Murphy had primed her well, and at this rate it wouldn't take much to set her off.

With her eyes covered, her other senses seemed to sharpen. The smell of the outdoors came on strong. They were not walking on concrete or pavement anymore. In fact she swore she scented pine needles. She'd not paid attention for a second to the trip here, so she had no idea how long they'd been in the car or where they could have gone. Maybe Chase had a cabin or something she didn't know about.

A sudden breeze kicked up and brushed across Eve's skin. Wherever they were, there was a lot of humidity and… She inhaled deeply through her nose.

"Are we at the lake?" Chase and Murphy shared a condo downtown, and as far as she knew they owned no property at the lake. Hadn't Murphy told her that Chase did not like the water at all? Not even in a swimming pool.

Chase didn't respond to her question other than to tighten his arm around her waist and lead her forward. The tension in Eve coiled tight. Arousal be damned, suddenly being blindfolded and led to God knew what frightened her. A shiver worked down her spine.

"Easy, girl. You're fine."

Eve focused on Chase's voice and relaxed a fraction. She loved the way he and Murphy made her feel when they were like this. They demanded and took what they wanted, but never forgot to reassure or comfort her when she needed it. Those little moments meant the world to her and were the crux of why she was willing to give them so much trust.

He stopped moving, and her breath clogged her throat. Was this it? He spun her around, and someone grabbed her wrist. Murphy she presumed. What if it wasn't him? They'd not discussed including anyone else, but then again she'd not bothered with many questions when she'd agreed to this. She'd given them permission to do as they pleased.

Eve wanted to explore her sexuality and learn if she had it in her to be what these two men needed. Still, logic fought with the need burning in her gut. Somehow she had to put aside her concerns and consider them—the two men she'd said she trusted.

Chase stepped away from her and her other cuff was grabbed as well. The clang of chains hitting metal made her flinch. Her arms were pulled taut over her head to the very edge of uncomfortable. A few minutes later the hands at her wrists disappeared and she remained in position, arms stretched high and wide. She gave a testing pull and got nowhere. Her wrists were securely shackled and her ability to protect herself completely stripped away.

"Spread your legs," Murphy murmured in her ear. "Slightly more than shoulder-width apart."

She only hesitated for a few seconds before she followed his instructions to the letter. Two hands quickly went to work at each of her ankles. First leather was wrapped around them, the sensation eerily similar to the handcuffs at her wrist. Then a cool metal bar was pressed to the inside of her thigh.

"I'm attaching a spreader bar. This will keep your legs open at the perfect angle so I'll be able to see that juicy pussy of yours at any given moment. There will be nothing you can hide from us."

Her stomach jumped. She wanted to see his eyes. See the lust she hoped burned inside him as much as it did her. Murphy leaned into her back. She knew it was him by the scent of his musk. She didn't need her eyes to tell him and Chase apart. Lips brushed across hers for a brief second. Chase. A hot taste from a wild man who kept his control on such a tight leash, she wondered what would happen when he let it free.

"Thank you for this," Murphy whispered.

She relaxed against the chains, grateful for his presence. She arched her neck in an eager display for another kiss from the man who'd moved out of her reach.

Instead cool metal slid across her neck. Not a round shaft but a sharp edge scraping against her. Eve froze. The cry lodged in the back of her throat. *Oh God, please tell me he does not have a knife.*

The sharp, flat edge sank a millimeter into her flesh. Her heart beat wildly. He didn't break the skin or hurt her. She only felt the pressure of the now warm blade.

"I suspect it will take some time and more than a few punishments for you to truly feel the trust we need from you. Although tonight is a very good start." The rough edge of Murphy's voice shivered across her skin. The underlying tone of his statement was a clear reprimand. Something told her she was in for a punishment tonight.

With the knife at her throat keeping her perfectly still, Murphy used his free hand to slide into her pussy. "I'm not sure how it's possible, but I think you're even wetter than in the car." He shoved two fingers into her opening, and she gasped at the sensation. The near-constant ache around her clit intensified. Fresh moisture flooded between her legs, and Murphy groaned in her ear.

"Tonight you'll be my lovely little slut, won't you?"

She'd be anything for him if he'd stop the teasing and get on with the pleasing.

"You'll take my cock in your mouth, your hot little cunt, and even up your ass if it's what I want, won't you?" When she didn't answer right away, the blade pressed deeper into her skin, creating a sharp sting.

Desire for everything he spoke of pushed Eve past the glimmer of fear still pressing at her mind. "Yes, Sir. I'll be your slut."

Murphy repeated the in-and-out motions with his fingers in her pussy. Buried to the hilt one minute and rimming the opening another. Eve pumped her hips into his hand, but the metal pressing against her flesh inhibited her movements.

"Be still," he ordered. His hand slid from her wetness. Her cries of displeasure went ignored. Until two fingers slick with her own juices were pushed between her buttocks and into the tight hole of her ass. This time her cries weren't of agony, but an extreme bliss when Murphy rubbed across unused nerve endings.

The sound of the camera clicking penetrated the lust haze around her brain but meant nothing to her. Ferocious need seized her body and brain until she thought she might explode from it. All conscious though centered between her legs and the achy and swollen flesh that needed more attention.

"God, I could fuck you right now."

"Yes, please. Please, Sir, fuck me. Fuck me."

With no warning, a hard rap of fingers struck her clit, slapping the mound of her pussy. Shock and sensation vibrated through her as the heat of Chase covered her front.

"How can you not see your submissive nature?"

Eve shook her head. "Stop saying that."

Murphy's fingers pushed deeper, igniting the pathways with more pleasure than she'd experienced before.

"Jesus, Eve. It's not a bad thing. It's a wondrous, beautiful thing to see a woman embrace her nature and submit to a dominant." Chase moved away, and the sudden sound of the camera clicking thundered in her ears.

With fingers buried to the hilt, Murphy released the knife from her neck and moved it to her front. "I hope you weren't too attached to this dress."

Before she could respond, the blade sliced through the fabric from sternum to belly. She'd forgone panties but insisted on the bra. Now the knife slid under the strap and pulled it away from her body. The squeak left her throat at the same time the bra opened and her ample tits spilled from their confines.

The knife disappeared, as did Murphy's fingers from her bottom. For long minutes the only thing she heard was the sound of her own heavy breathing as she hung from the chains. Fear crept its way back into her mind. She was bound and helpless with no control over what happened next.

Only the knowledge that Murphy and Chase watched over her kept her from freaking out. She would not be forgotten. There was a bond of belief — of need — that linked them all together. She didn't fully understand, but deep down her gut believed.

Still, the ever-present sliver of fear did not go away. She tried to fight against the bindings at both her wrists and ankles to no avail.

"You aren't going anywhere and neither are we." Chase's voice even at a distance reassured her.

"We'd never leave you," Murphy vowed behind her before placing his palm across her right breast. The heat of his touch warmed like a brand to her skin. Safety, she reminded herself. Chase and Murphy meant safe.

Murphy's hand slid around her torso to cup the underside of her left breast. His other hand soon followed. With his front pressed to her back, Eve rested her head on his chest and arched her chest forward in invitation for him to do more. He ignored her.

"Everything about you is so responsive. Especially these nipples. I haven't even touched them yet and they stand to attention begging for me. They need to be clamped."

Eve whimpered at the thought. A sharp sliver of want sliced through her at every word he spoke. His fingers stayed on the move, tracing first one tight bud and then the next. She wanted to cry in frustration when he did everything but squeeze the aching points.

"Sometime soon I'll bind them. Experiment with different ways to torture your tits until you're begging me to fuck you. Then when I do, I'll take the pain further one inch at a time until you gush all over my dick."

Eve's pussy clenched at his descriptions. Sweat broke out across her skin, and more want and desire than she thought possible squeezed in her stomach.

"Please, Sir."

"Yes, Eve. Beg me, baby. It won't do you any good right now, but it's music to my ears."

Tears threatened to spill on her checks. Eve squeezed her eyes shut tight to stave them off. The demand for release clawed at her insides like a beast desperate to get free, and she suspected they'd barely begun to deny her.

"Believe it or not, tonight isn't going to be about denial. Not exactly." At his words, he grabbed her nipples and twisted them. Pain shot twin arrows through her body and straight toward her clit. Her gasp only encouraged him to twist harder. Additional pinpricks of pain assailed her. Eve whimpered.

"C'mon, Eve. Take the pain. Take it for both Chase and me. We know you can."

Eve gritted her teeth and did as he asked. The thought of letting him down now devastated her.

Murphy attacked her neck with his mouth, alternating kisses and sharp little bites at the curve between shoulder and neck. The stings of the bites were quickly washed away by the intense waves of pleasure with each flick of his tongue. This time she moaned into it, and he finally released the tight hold on her nipples.

She'd be sore tomorrow, but she wanted him to do it again. Automatically she arched toward his hands, and his rich laughter rumbled against her throat.

"That's what I thought."

She had no idea what she'd turned into in his arms, but she desperately wanted to embrace it. Her deepest, darkest fantasies were bubbling to the surface, anxious to be fulfilled.

Murphy repeated the pull on her nipples, and this time Eve let the scream loose from her throat. Her body warred with the decision between pain and pleasure until it gave in to every demand Murphy made. She wanted nothing more than to be taken. To be filled by them both and allowed to come over and over again.

Suddenly a hand wrapped around her throat. Not Murphy. He still played with her nipples. *Chase*. The name whispered in her mind a second before he spoke.

"You need to be fucked." His hand tightened against her windpipe and fresh fear gripped her.

"Chase!" she cried out, her hands yanking on the chains that held her.

"That's not what you call him anymore." Murphy's fingers tightened the twist of her nipples as he spoke.

"Sir," she panted. It was the only word she could get out.

"Relax and take shallow breaths. You're fine as long as you don't panic."

Panic? Was he kidding? Still, she did the best she could to tamp down the rising anxiety.

Chase lowered his free hand to the mound of her sex. At first he simply cupped her sensitive flesh, driving her mad. The possessive grip on her throat and pussy had her more aroused than ever before. She couldn't fathom how that was possible.

Her sex clenched in aching need. The want to be filled overwhelmed her every thought. "Please, Chase," she whispered. His fingers lessened slightly to allow her words. "Need to see."

She felt Murphy move behind her, and he lifted her blindfold. Eve squinted against the lights shining in her face. Spots formed in her vision, and she winced when Chase's hand tightened once again.

Eve eased her eyes open and focused on Chase looming in front of her. Her first glance at his eyes revealed the single most important thing she needed to see from him. Desire so strong it took her breath away. The standard hard look on his face had been softened with his own need riding him hard.

She'd done this. Secret satisfaction warmed her soul. This was exactly what she'd read about, and now she finally understood. Submission wasn't weak, it was powerful. She'd said yes to his desires and he'd revealed a need for her she was certain no one had ever felt before.

Murphy leaned into her back, his mouth at her right ear. "You're our girl now. Our slut to do anything we want with."

Eve moaned. His words caused the ache in her clit to intensify. They were going to torture her to death with pleasure. Hot fingers dug into the skin of her hips, holding her in place for Chase's explorations. Sensation after sensation layered atop her already on-fire nerve endings. Much more and she'd explode like a fireball, whether they wanted her to or not.

Hands roamed her body while the intensity continued to build. The ache had gone beyond what she thought she could bear. None of that mattered anymore. Whatever they did, whatever they asked, she would give them. Anything they wanted. She trusted that when they were good and ready they'd see to her satisfaction. They would decide when the time was right for her.

Something snapped inside her. This wasn't about one night at all. She wanted—no, needed—to belong.

"Yours." The harsh whisper of her voice barely made it past the hold Chase maintained on her. But she knew the second he comprehended the word. His eyes widened slightly, and his jaw ground tighter.

Immediately his hand dropped from her throat and he lowered to her mouth. He devoured her with a kiss so out of control, so soul searing, she knew it would never be forgotten, no matter what the future brought her.

She belonged to Chase and Murphy, and nothing and no one could take that away from her.

He dropped to his knees. The heat of his breath caressed her wet and swollen folds. Chase leaned forward, his mouth hovering less than an inch from where she needed it. If her hands had been free, she'd have been tempted to grab his head and pull him to her. Or even take matters into her own hands. She could only imagine the kind of punishment she'd be in for then.

"Submissive."

This time when he said the word, she cried out, "Yes!"

"Do you want to be fucked?"

"Yes, please."

"Who, Eve. Tell me who you want to fill your holes and ease the ache."

His crude words reacted to her need like gasoline on a slow-simmering fire. The resulting meltdown left her unable to speak. She was about to blow, and Chase had not moved an inch closer.

Chase's laughter brushed air across her cunt before he stood and faced her. "You're almost ready."

Almost! Her mind screamed the word she couldn't say. Her body arched in his direction, pulling at the cuffs buckled to her wrists. Maybe she could entice him to finish the job.

A hard *thwack* across her naked buttocks brought her up short. "Don't go getting naughty now. We control this situation, little Eve, not you." Murphy was back at her ear, whispering words that sent bolts of electricity straight to her clit.

Chase picked up his camera and resumed taking pictures. Had it not been for the hard line of his jaw and the massive erection bulging in his pants, she would have thought he'd blown her off.

Another solid smack on her ass brought her back to Murphy at her ear. Somehow the pain in her rear didn't scare her or curb her arousal. If anything, it intensified it. Although how she could get any more needy she couldn't fathom.

"Please fuck me," she begged.

"Eventually we will. When we're ready."

To her surprise, Murphy reached between her thighs and swiped through her moisture a few times before he slid through the crease of her ass and pushed his lubricated fingers inside her small entrance. The stretching and burning came faster this time than before. He had to be using more fingers to stretch her wider. He wanted to prepare her for when they took her at the same time.

The sensation of fullness became intense as he tunneled forward. The moment she thought she'd hit the limit of what she could take, he dragged his fingers back out and elicited a streak of pleasure so extreme she nearly passed out.

She wanted to grind down on his fingers and do it again, but the restraints kept her unable to do so.

"You want more, don't you?"

She nodded furiously.

With what had to be the most wicked intent, he drove his fingers to the hilt.

Eve moaned.

"Time to make you scream for the camera, baby girl." Murphy tilted his fingers inside her and started a slow easy drag from her body. Then he did it all over again.

Eve clawed at the chains holding her nearly immobile while Murphy manipulated her backside. Her pending orgasm coiled behind her clit, waiting impatiently to strike when she least expected it. The wait was maddening.

One more stroke in and out of her snug rear channel, and she couldn't take it anymore. Her entire body trembled uncontrollably. Pleasure swamped her.

"Tell us who you want to fuck you, and I'll make you come harder than you've ever come before."

"You and Chase. Please…"

"No!" His fingers pushed harder inside her.

"You, Sir and Chase, Sir."

"Close, but no cigar."

Eve couldn't think. What did he want from her?

Patient to the end, Murphy silently finger fucked her ass. When the pleasure infused with new burning, she'd have sworn he added another finger. The buildup between her legs drove her crazy. She had to come now before it was too late.

"Say it." He curled an arm around her hip and gave her clit a hard rub. "Who do you belong to?"

"Both of you."

"And what are we?"

Finally she understood what he wanted. "My masters. Oh my God, you're my masters!" She yelled the last word into the lens of Chase's camera as he moved close, taking picture after picture.

The second Murphy's fingers touched her clit again, the heat between her legs exploded. The resulting fireball ripped through her and melted her brain. Pain blended with pleasure into an incredible wave of bliss she couldn't begin to understand.

Screams tore from her throat as her head tumbled into the darkness of Murphy and Chase. When the convulsions subsided, Murphy eased from her body and wrapped both arms around her waist to support her.

Chase immediately went to work on releasing the chains from her wrists. First one, then the other. Too weak to hold herself up, she leaned into Murphy even farther.

Perfection ensconced her. Her heartbeat pounded wildly as she tried to focus on her surroundings. She'd never dreamed they'd push her this far and she would end up loving it. And she did. Every single second.

Chase knelt at her feet to unfasten the bar holding her legs open. In some distant part of her brain she knew everything ached. That she'd not be able to walk on her own for a little while. None of that mattered though. Weakly she managed to lean slightly forward. Enough to run her fingers through the soft strands of Chase's dark hair. She had two masters now. Something she'd never dreamed would happen to her.

Her beautiful photographer lifted his head, his gaze meeting hers, and the tension she saw sucked the air from her lungs. Chase was not happy. The rough lines etched in his forehead drew deep. Irritation and something she didn't understand stared back at her.

What had she done?

"Jesus, Murphy, get her in the car."

Eve turned away from his scorn and hid her face in Murphy's chest when he lifted her into his arms. She fought against the need to cry to no avail. Hot, wet tears rolled down her cheeks and onto Murphy's skin.

When they reached the car, she twisted in Chase's direction for one last look. Maybe she'd misread his feelings.

He still stood where she'd been restrained, the chains and bar still in his hands. The anger in his face had not diminished as he watched her being taken away.

Her cheeks heated with a cross between shame and disappointment. Eve swore for as long as she lived she'd never forget the pained scowl she made out in the darkness.

THIRTEEN

The desolation in Eve's chest threatened to break her. How could she have been so wrong? And why the hell did they do this to her if it bothered Chase so much?

It had been all about the pictures. The reminder zinged through her mind in startling clarity. She was such a fucking idiot. He'd warned her more than once how things would go. There'd been no denying how much he wanted to photograph her, which inevitably led to fucking. It was her fault for fooling herself into thinking it had meant more.

Still, they'd demanded she face her true nature against all her objections. And she had. Like it or not, she couldn't deny her submissiveness. But what if it was something she'd only felt for Chase and Murphy?

Jesus, Eve. Two men. Seriously? Who takes that seriously?

Apparently she did.

A fresh bout of shame filled her. Her naïveté astounded even her. Now she just wanted to close her eyes and cry until she got it all out. Maybe then she could look at the situation objectively. Eve sighed. More tears would do her no good at this point. Even embarrassed anger couldn't overcome the exhaustion threatening to claim her.

She needed to get home—and fast. With startling clarity she remembered whose arms still cuddled her close. Murphy had taken her to the car, covered her in a blanket, and all without a single word. She'd gotten so lost in her own shameful thoughts, she'd momentarily forgotten him.

Now she became hyperaware of his heat blanketing her. His distinct and woodsy smell that always made her feel so good. And the hard jean-covered cock pressing against the curves of her ass.

It dawned on her that while they'd blown her mind in release, neither of them had tried to fuck her yet. If Murphy wanted to take her now, there really wasn't much she could do to stop him. She still craved a connection, and being cast aside so easily by Chase left her more vulnerable than ever.

She tensed in his arms, worried where things would lead. "I want to go home."

"We will soon enough." His dick twitched under her.

The smooth, commanding voice he used with her heightened her awareness. She couldn't go through with this. "No, you don't understand. I have to get away. Now."

"Relax, Eve. It's not what you think. Don't lose faith now." His hand smoothed her hair and stroked her back.

What the hell was that supposed to mean? "Don't tell me to relax. Just take me home." Maybe she'd apologize later when she wasn't mortally embarrassed or as weak as a newborn.

"Don't tempt me, Eve. I need to fuck and you don't. However, my self-control only goes so far with the gorgeous naked woman I desire the most squirming on my lap."

Oh! He wouldn't. Would he? She quit moving immediately. Despite the emotional turmoil roiling through her, a shocking blast of arousal flamed bright, embarrassing her even further. She had to be defective even to think about him that way now. But it wasn't Murphy who'd rejected her.

New tears pooled in her eyes. The hot shame of Chase's rejection filled her once again.

Murphy pulled her head to his chest again. "Don't worry, little one. You've had more than enough for one night. My only intention is to take you home and make sure you rest."

Eve sighed into him. She didn't have the energy to fight or worry. Tomorrow she'd deal with the fallout. For now, she had Murphy.

"As for Chase..." Murphy hesitated. "There are things you don't know about him—about us."

Now he'd gone and piqued her curiosity. Although why she cared she had no idea.

"He'll come to his senses later, and then he's going to feel like a jackass."

Good. She wanted him to suffer just like she was.

Eve sighed. She wasn't a spiteful person and she didn't want to be one now. If Chase didn't want her, so be it. She was a grown woman fully capable of accepting that whatever she'd thought had been there simply wasn't. Still, the memories of the scene flooded her mind. She'd likely regret how it ended, but nothing could take that kind of pleasure away from her. For a few minutes she'd been at peace. Something that had eluded her until now.

Now she'd have to figure out how to get it on her own. It's what she did. Face reality and find her own escapes. The little pleasures that made her forget the bad or the mundane.

Eve yawned.

"Try not to take Chase too personally tonight. He swore he wouldn't get involved in another ménage relationship ever again. Now he's half in love and it pisses him off."

She snorted. "Half in love? You're crazy. Did you see the look he gave me? That was not the look of a man half in love."

Murphy lowered his lips to her ear. "I might be crazy, but when it comes to Chase, I know exactly what I'm talking about. You'll see."

Eve shook her head. She didn't want to see. Accepting her mistake had to be the first step to getting past all of this. Murphy was a gentle soul. A demanding, deviant soul, but gentle with emotions as well. She would miss him after tonight. She'd have to quit her job and start looking for new employment all over again. That was definitely going to suck.

"Sleep now, Eve. You think too much." He brushed a chaste kiss across her cheek and patted her hip.

Maybe when she woke up she'd find herself at home and realize all of this was a dream.

Wait. She jerked her head up.

"Did you say another ménage relationship?"

Murphy laughed. "A little slow on the uptake. That's the kind of thing that can happen after an intense scene. Yeah, I said another."

"When? What? Who?" She couldn't form a coherent question.

"Sleep first. Then Chase can explain it to you. We need a submissive like you—he just hasn't accepted it yet."

Eve frowned. Yeah right. Chase wouldn't be talking to her anytime soon. And that word again. He'd forced her to accept it, to embrace that she needed to submit to them, and look what good it did her.

Grateful that at least Murphy had not abandoned her, she once again snuggled into him until she found a comfortable position that didn't stretch any of her already taxed-out muscles. On a sleepy sigh, she inhaled deeply. She wanted to imprint his scent on her memory. She had a feeling she would need it in the future when things got rocky.

Tomorrow she'd face the changes and start working on a new plan. Maybe she'd even find the courage to talk to her stepdad about the building she loved to hate. Either he gave her the control to restore it the way it needed to be, or she'd walk away. A fresh change was definitely in order.

* * *

Chase sat at Eve's kitchen table in the dark. He'd waited for Murphy to come and ream him a new one. But the hours passed, and he never heard him stir from her bedroom. Good for him. At least one of them had their priorities straight.

They should have both spent their night cherishing the woman who'd surrendered fully to them for the first time ever. He'd pushed her right along with Murphy, determined to make her understand who she was and that it was okay to embrace.

She'd done it and he'd been damned proud of her. Still was. No woman had ever tempted him like she did. Not even Cynthia. Chase sighed. When was he going to give it up and stop letting another woman's betrayal fester in his gut? He cared far more for Eve, and he'd rejected her in a heartbeat.

Murphy had gone too far when he'd made her admit they were her masters. He might be a shit right now, but Murphy wasn't completely blameless. He'd warned him not to try and make this a relationship for the three of them. Playtime was one thing, anything more was out of the question.

So then why did the thought of Murphy in there with her alone burn him from the inside out? He should have left and gone home hours ago. He'd been given an out and he damn sure needed to take it. Yet here he still sat. Waiting for Murphy to call him out.

"I'm keeping her for myself."

Chase bristled at the words Murphy uttered. "Like hell you are."

"Do you have any idea what your behavior tonight did to her? It's going to take a hell of a lot of maneuvering on my part to even convince her to let me stay in her life. You are a fucking prick."

Chase winced at Murphy's not incorrect assessment.

"I finally get it, okay? You don't want to have a relationship that includes both of us with her. Fine. Have it your way. But I'm keeping her, so you'd better get used to it."

Chase shoved his chair away from the table and stood. Anger fired his blood, and jealousy drove him insane. "No."

"Fuck you, Chase. You aren't the boss this time. You relinquished that right about six hours ago in a fucking public park." Murphy moved forward, fists clenched at his side.

"This isn't about you."

"The hell it's not. It's about you, it's about me, and it's about Eve. The woman we broke tonight deserved so much better than you gave her."

Red-hot rage burst free in Chase's head. He swung his fist and connected with Murphy's jaw. Pain exploded in his hand, and Murphy's head swung back. Chase welcomed the pain, the torn skin on his fists, and the anger he saw reflected in Murphy's eyes.

"You son of a bitch." Murphy charged him, grabbing him at the waist and driving him back into the wall. Dishes rattled and crashed from the counter to the floor, and still Chase saw nothing but the thick haze of jealousy. He couldn't simply give Eve to Murphy. It would eat him alive to be left out.

"What the hell?" Eve stepped into the room. "Murphy, Chase, what the hell are you doing to my kitchen?"

Murphy froze on top of him, fist poised in midair. Eve ran toward them.

"Stop!" they yelled in unison.

She halted her progress but continued to glare.

"There's glass, baby. I don't want you to get hurt." Murphy's tone changed instantly with Eve. Protective.

"Me? Are you kidding? You don't want me hurt, but it's okay to pummel each other?" She backed out of the room and disappeared around the corner.

Murphy turned back to him, anger and hurt still etched in his features. Before either of them spoke, Eve sauntered back into the kitchen with a pair of slippers on her feet and a broom in her hand.

"Are you two done breaking my things?" Resignation had settled in her voice, and it tore at Chase's gut. He'd done this to her.

He jumped from the floor and lunged for the broom. "Let me."

She yanked it out of his grasp. "Haven't you done enough tonight?" She swept at the glass and porcelain shards scattered across the floor.

"I fucked up."

Her sweeping halted, but she kept her head down and eyes averted. At least he had her attention.

"I don't know what I was thinking. I didn't expect—" Fuck. Who was he kidding? He couldn't lie to her now.

"Don't bother, Chase. You told me from the beginning this was a bad idea. It was a job. One I agreed to do and then be done. We both knew it would lead to sex. Just leave it at that."

Chase grabbed her and hauled her against him. "Sex. You think this was just about getting laid?" He tightened his fingers around her arms like tight bands. The need to hold her still and make her listen was all that mattered. "I knew the minute you walked by me the very first time with your fuck-me shoes and feminine swagger that you'd mean more than someone to fuck. Your scent alone had the power to send me to my office to jack off every damn day. I've been falling for you ever since."

She struggled against his hold. He clamped tighter. He wasn't letting her go. Not now that his heart was on the line. "But, baby, I see the way you look at us both and I've been down that road before, and you don't want to go there. Trust me."

"Why? Because that's what happened to you the last time?"

Her words shocked him to his core. Of course, Murphy told her. He'd undermined this relationship from the get-go. "Yes." He had nothing more to offer on that subject.

"So, you're scared. Big deal."

The fire in her eyes singed his pride. "Not scared. Realistic. There's a difference."

"Whatever."

Chase roughly released her, and Eve stumbled back a few steps. "Easy for you to say, I guess. You're not the one who spent a year wondering what had gone wrong. Why out of the blue the woman we cared about turned into a jealous psycho hell bent on ruining everything about us. A fucking year where I used women like she'd used us."

"What!" she shrieked. "Easy?" She took two steps and stopped with only a few inches between them. "You think what happened tonight was easy? I gave you and Murphy something I never thought I'd give to anyone. Not after the shit I've been through." She poked him in his chest.

He grabbed her finger and walked her backward until her butt hit the edge of the table he'd spent the night sitting at. "Don't."

"Don't what? Tell you the truth?"

"Don't push me." A fierce need already grabbed him by the balls, urging him to take what he wanted and fuck the consequences. He needed her at that moment as much as he needed his next breath.

"Maybe I wasn't the only one who needed to be pushed. But we both have to give up the pain of the past or this has to end now." The warmth of her breath caressed the front of his face. Sweet Lord, this woman would be his undoing.

"I won't let you go." If he took her now, it would seal their fate. There'd be no turning back. He closed his eyes. "I can't let you go."

"Thank you, Sir."

Her shocking acceptance broke him. Logic be damned.

Chase grabbed her wrists and brought her arms behind her. With both of her hands at the small of her back, he wrapped one of his much larger hands around them both and clasped them together. His dominant need to overpower her made things a little rough, but the hot gleam in her gaze indicated her appreciation. She loved to be restrained.

He pushed his thigh between her legs and pressed against her sex. The flimsy T-shirt she'd worn to sleep in did little to hide the heat building between her legs. Chase leaned over her, pressing her back close to the table.

"Do you want me to fuck you?"

"Oh God, yes. Please."

The husky whisper fueled his intent. He loved hearing her breathless.

He made quick work of unfastening his pants and shoving them past his hips. He pushed the fabric of her shirt out of his way and reveled in the sight of her swollen and juicy cunt. The proof of how much she wanted him glistened across her silky, bare folds. With a tight fist around the hard length of his cock, he thrust to the hilt, forcing his way inside her tight channel. Nothing soft or easy this time. He had to take. Claim. Conquer.

His savage in-and-out rhythm began before she even had a chance to take a breath. Blind need drove his movements despite the flood of emotions he felt for this woman. He had no intention of hurting her, only giving them both what they truly needed.

"You belong to me too," he growled.

"Yes. Oh yes, Master," she moaned. Her cries of pleasure grew louder every time he yanked on her wrists to tighten his hold.

"Take it," he grated, the civil veneer long gone. "You are mine. Mine to fuck. Mine to punish as I see fit. And mine to share."

"Oohh," she moaned louder.

His dick swelled. Everything about her was so perfect. The sheen of perspiration glistening on her skin, the lush curves of her body so soft under his hands. He couldn't lose her.

"Oh God, Chase," she cried. The vise grip of her channel on his dick told him just how close she was to the edge.

"I will fuck this pussy whenever and wherever I want."

"Yes. Fuck, yes." She screamed in surrender as the release hammered through her. She arched under him, her muscles pulling at his dick.

Still, he fucked her harder. "I love you like this, Eve. So wet and needy. Coming all over my dick." Her eyes grew wide while he watched her tumble into another soul-gripping orgasm that pulled him under as well.

He impaled her one last time in an urgent and powerful thrust, losing himself inside her.

"Jesus Christ," he gasped, pressing his forehead to the sweet curve of her neck. He lifted her slightly and released her arms. In a slow, languid move she eased her arms to her sides. She'd be sore later, but it'd been worth it. He'd needed to push hard, and she'd not only accepted it, but reveled in it. Now he needed more.

"Eve?" He lifted his head so he could watch her eyes. See her reaction to his words.

"Yes, Chase?" The sweet smile delivered with the question tumbled his stomach. He wanted to wake up to that every morning from here on out.

"Come home with us."

FOURTEEN

Eve checked her appearance in the dressing-room mirror one more time. Today's shoot had been long and grueling, in more ways than one.

She'd spent the last few days and nights ensconced in Chase and Murphy's condo, barely able to get out of bed. Their sexual appetites never gave her a moment's peace, and she'd loved every second of it. The few times they'd had to leave the bedroom long enough to take care of work-related issues, they'd tied or bound her in a manner that left her little to do but wait for them to return. Surprisingly, she'd actually enjoyed the freedom that had given her.

With no responsibilities beyond her training, she'd had plenty of time to contemplate the changes in her life. She'd fallen hard and fast for two men, and despite the emotions and desire involved, she had needed that time to come to terms with not only their expectations but hers as well.

It warmed her through to know that her masters understood this. They'd shared with her their pain from their last shared relationship, and she'd opened up about the fucked-up relationship between her stepdad and her mother that had colored her view of relationships from the get-go.

Today she'd returned to work. As much as she'd enjoyed the modeling, it wasn't what she wanted to do full-time. They'd agreed that her talents were more useful to them in other ways, plus they'd gotten greedy over whom they allowed to see her pictures. The pictures they'd taken in the park had been unbelievable.

Chase's talent captured every moment of her breaking down exquisitely, and she'd agreed with them that they were far too personal to share with the world. Save for a few.

One of the shots of Murphy with a knife at her throat had been so good, she'd encouraged Chase to use it in an upcoming show she'd decided to host for them.

When Chase had pointed out how close her building was to the arts district and many of the local art galleries, she'd gotten an immediate idea. Why not renovate the building using her signature shabby chic style and create a gallery and a studio on the first floor, some hand picked complimentary businesses on the second, and a few select and very expensive living apartments on the third?

All of which had led to today's photo shoot. Chase had suggested the place needed to include pinup artwork, an idea she'd embraced. Until he'd insisted she be the focus. Old insecurities flared their ugly heads, something she'd spent the last eight hours tamping down.

Murphy had hired an assistant for the day to take care of the clothing and makeup, and even brought in Jennifer as a second model. Eve stood transfixed in front of the mirror. Even after seeing herself made-up several times now, she was still amazed by the transformation. She really did look like a '50s pinup girl.

Her hair had been pinned into a sleek and slightly poofy old-fashioned do, and her makeup applied thick and colorful. Eve rubbed her hands down the fine bones of the striped and fringed corset. She'd fallen in love with it at first sight and already planned to buy one as soon as she got to her computer.

The long pencil skirt seemed demure, but atop black fishnet stockings and patent leather platform heels, it screamed sexy kitten. To top off the look, they'd applied temporary tattoo sleeves to both her arms. She'd always been curious about ink, and she liked the edgy look it added to the ensemble. So much so that she considered asking Chase and Murphy if she could get a real tattoo.

"They're asking for you, darlin'." Jennifer walked into the room and collapsed into the makeup chair. "I'm beat."

Eve didn't blame her. They'd both been here since early this morning, and Chase and Murphy had used them well. After today she figured they must have gone easy on her before.

"The pictures are going to be awesome, though. I can't wait to see the new gallery." Jennifer reached for her stilettos and removed them. Immediately she began massaging her feet.

"It's still going to be a while. We've barely begun the design stage. Next week I have to start interviewing contractors."

"Ooh, hunky guys in work boots. Can I come watch?"

Eve laughed. "Like you need any more men clamoring after you. You probably have to beat them off."

A flash of sadness clouded Jennifer's eyes for a split second before she grinned back. "You'd be surprised. You'd better get out there before they come looking for you. Those two men do *not* like to be kept waiting." Jennifer winked.

"Yeah, I'm beginning to learn that. I'll talk to you later." Eve left the dressing room with an odd twinge in her stomach. For a second there she could have sworn Jennifer looked...unhappy.

Quietly she opened the door to the studio, tiptoeing on her toes to keep the noise down. If Chase was in the middle of something, she didn't want to disturb him with her heels clacking on the wood floor.

Whatever he was doing, it required soft lighting, because all of the lights were turned out except for the soft glow coming from behind the partition. Eve turned the corner and came to a shocked standstill at the scene before her. They'd moved the wrought-iron bed front and center again and lit candles. Dozens and dozens of them. The flickering flames cast various shadows around the room, highlighting the romantic scene her men had set.

"What's all this?"

Chase and Murphy turned in her direction, hot intent coming from both their gazes.

"Stand right there and don't move," Chase commanded.

Eve crinkled her forehead and shifted her stance. "Chase, I don't think—"

"That's right. You don't think." He approached her like a wild animal hunting prey. Hard lines and muscle moving in her direction.

Need built in her pussy and immediately dampened her folds.

"Yes, Sir," she uttered, totally fascinated by the onset of their need. She liked when they came at her out of the blue. Sometimes at home, Murphy was known to grab her in the kitchen, bend her over the table, and push his hot cock into her. It always shocked her how much she enjoyed those fast and wild couplings. He'd watched Chase fuck her in her kitchen the night they fought, and admitted watching her be dominated by Chase had been a huge turn-on.

"Good girl." Murphy approached her slowly with black rope in his hands.

Her insides trembled. Would she always react this way when they restrained her? God, she hoped so.

"Show me your wrists."

Eve did as he asked, holding them out in front of her. She was too damned turned on to even consider not obeying. The fact she trusted them both implicitly gave her a huge confidence boost.

He wrapped the soft rope around her skin, binding her hands together. She wiggled her fingers, and as usual he'd used the perfect amount of tension to keep her blood flowing while making it impossible for her to get free. Push come to shove, she might be able to use her teeth to loosen the knots, but she doubted it. The man was a master at bondage.

Once her wrists were bound, Murphy traced his fingers along her jawline. "You're very beautiful, Eve. And you did a great job today."

Her stomach flip-flopped. "Thank you, Sir."

"I don't think you understand how crazy I am about you. But you will." He replaced his finger with his lips and kissed a trail from jaw to shoulder until she shuddered against him. Apparently satisfied, he nipped at her skin with teeth. Sharp little bites that didn't break the skin but sent slivers of sensation racing to her clit.

Her breath accelerated and her heart raced. *More.* Oh she wanted so much more.

Murphy moved around behind her, and she stood immobile now, staring into the depth of Chase's heated gaze. Warm fingers settled at the small of her back, stroking the small space between the edge of the corset and the waistband of her skirt. The subtle tease drove her wild. When she wanted to scream for more, Murphy finally undid the button on her skirt and slid the zipper down.

Chase lifted his camera and took a few shots while Murphy undressed her.

"As much as I love the corset, it's got to go. I want to see your pretty pink nipples." He pulled the laces and loosened the corset and Chase stepped forward to undo the front. Cool air stroked across her skin, tightening her already aching nipples.

Moments later she stood simply clad in fishnet stockings and high heels. She hadn't been given thigh highs for the shoot today, so her pussy was still covered, albeit by a wide-open weave of netting.

Chase and Murphy looked at each other and her legs. Obviously they had the same idea as she did. They would have to come off as well. To her surprise, neither made a move to remove them. Instead Chase's fingers dived at her pussy, and Murphy eased between the cheeks of her ass.

"No, these won't be coming off. They're too damned hot, but adjustments do have to be made."

Before she responded, they ripped at the threads and her body jerked between them. In a matter of seconds her normal stockings became crotchless.

"Now we have access to both holes," Chase mocked.

His crude words didn't offend her. Quite the opposite. The more dirty talk, the wetter she became, and he damned well knew it. They were going to draw this out and tease her to the brink of madness. She could feel the truth of it all the way to her core.

"Are you ready for this, baby?"

Eve shivered at Murphy's whisper at her ear. He had a way of reaching into her soul and seeing her true feelings.

"Anything, Sir."

"And a safe word?"

"I don't need it." Tension eased from her muscles as they manipulated her body. She'd asked for this and waited impatiently to get it. Tonight she wanted both men penetrating her at the same time.

Murphy let out a deep breath. His warm breath blew across her neck while his hand traveled the curve of her waist and across the slope of her breast. Goose bumps rose along her arms. He followed with a hard pull on her nipple that zinged pleasure from her breast to her pussy. Her muscles clenched around Chase's fingers, eliciting a low moan from him.

Satisfaction. Yes. They controlled her pleasure; she created theirs.

"Tease me now and you'll find yourself across my knees with my belt burning your ass."

She groaned. Did he have any idea what his threats did to her? It took a force of will she barely had to obey him when the punishments sounded so delicious.

Chase thrust his fingers in her hair, pulling until the sharp pricks of pain blended with the pleasure of his fingers rubbing her clit. This time her moan was muffled when he crushed his mouth to hers. He thrust his tongue between her lips. Brute force shivered between them as he took what he needed.

When he broke free, she stood stunned from his intensity. She loved these men and their commanding ways.

"On the bed," Murphy demanded from behind her.

Chase stepped from in front of her and gestured toward the bed. "On your knees, head down."

Eve scrambled across the cool silk sheets and took up the position they desired. She raised her bound hands over her head and pressed her face into the mattress. With her ass thrust in the air, she waited for what was to come.

Big hands wrapped around her hips and dragged her toward the end of the bed. The mattress above her head dipped as one of them took a position in front of her.

Eve held her breath...waiting. What was coming next?

Slowly, her folds were parted and hot breath blew across her exposed flesh. A shudder of pleasure shook Eve's body. She tried to curl her hands into the sheets to no avail. Minutes passed and nothing changed. She was being held open for someone's view and nothing else.

Heat and need built in her core, and without thought she wiggled her hips in blatant invitation. A sharp bite to her buttocks followed, reminding her she was not in control. She couldn't help herself. The waiting drove her crazy, something they were fully aware of.

Cool air from the nearby fan caressed her aching flesh. Her heart raced, blood rushed to her pussy, and...one of their blazing hot tongues laved her sensitized skin from clit to anus.

She lifted her head on a gasp. Pleasure spiked and pressure mounted behind her clit. One more like that and she'd go off and earn herself another punishment.

A soft chuckle sounded near her head. "She likes that." Murphy. So Chase was the one lashing her with his wicked tongue.

He continued to lick her inflamed flesh. For a few minutes she fought against it, jerking away from his mouth. That only resulted in him grabbing her hips and holding her in place. Finally she gave in. She couldn't fight it anymore. The pleasure built. Insane. Sharp. Out of her control.

His thumb swiped her clit, and her hips bucked involuntarily. Tension coiled tight in her belly, threatening to snap at any moment. When he pushed two fingers into her opening, she whimpered her distress.

"Not yet, baby," Murphy murmured in her hair. "Not without permission."

"I can't control it."

"Yes, you can." Murphy's fingers threaded into her hair, tugging at the strands for distraction.

"Please…" she whimpered.

"Tell us what you want us to do and I'll consider it." Now Murphy wanted to play hardball.

"Both of you to take me. Now," she wailed.

"Oh please. Not good enough, Eve, and you know it."

Chase halted his movements.

Eve fought for breath. Composure.

"Please fuck me, Masters. Love me with both your cocks."

"Almost."

Eve shook her head in the sheets, humiliation hot on her face. "Please fuck my ass and my pussy — together."

For a few seconds silence filled the room before Chase sucked her clit into his mouth and fucked her with his fingers, hard. The ache of need sliced through her, overwhelming everything else. Pleasure swelled as she teetered on the edge.

"Come, Eve. Come for us now."

Murphy's words shocked and surprised her. She'd expected to be kept waiting tonight for a very long time.

While Chase plunged his fingers deep inside her, Murphy trailed his down her spine and in the crease of her ass. "This is going to be mine tonight."

The meaning of his words rasped over her. His thick cock would soon be pressing into her virgin hole. Even though she'd begged for it more than once, they'd said she wasn't ready. Murphy spread cool liquid across the small hole before dipping inside.

This pleasure she knew all too well. He took great satisfaction in preparing her for this every night. His finger worked past the tight ring of muscle, and Eve gave in to her need. Two fingers in her cunt, one in her ass, and one very hot tongue sucking on her clit were more than she could bear.

"Now, dammit."

Sound exploded in Eve's head. Screams from her own mouth as the intense buildup crested under Murphy's command. Chase lapped furiously at her release, gorging on her flesh while Murphy eased his fingers from her body.

Slowly, they brought her back down until her cries melted into whimpers and she collapsed on the bed.

"Goddamn our woman is wet." She could all but see the grin on Chase's smug face.

"Then I'd say she's ready." Murphy picked her up and cuddled her to his chest. He sealed his lips over hers, and she reveled in his familiar, comforting taste. Trepidation of what they were about to do wouldn't hold her back from the need swirling in the room. She wasn't the only one who needed it. They all did.

Murphy brushed a thumb across her nipple, sending a shock of hot desire coursing through her.

Chase lay on the bed and motioned to her with his hands. "Come here, baby."

She practically jumped out of Murphy's arms to obey. She wasn't even sure when Chase had removed his clothes, but there he was, all hard muscles and warm skin. He pulled her on top of him, and she rubbed her nose into his chest. He smelled good too. Different from Murphy but definitely a second delicious musk she wanted rubbed all over her.

The rigid length of his cock prodded her belly, reminding her what he desired. However, maneuvering with her hands bound was not easy. "A little help here," she pleaded.

"I don't want to wear a condom, Eve, ever again. I need to feel every sacred inch of you."

"Isn't it already a little late to worry about that now? Besides, I already told you I was on the pill. We're safe."

"And I'm clean," Chase whispered.

"Definitely me too." She wiggled her body against him. "I'd like you bare, Sir. Please."

Chase groaned, and Murphy must have taken that as his cue. He wrapped his hands around her waist and lifted her so Chase could place his cockhead at her entrance. Murphy lowered her one inch at a time, teasing her mercilessly.

She whimpered as the rigid flesh split her open and her muscles stretched to give him room. Eve bit her bottom lip and wriggled her hips, anything to create the friction she desired.

When Chase had fully impaled her and her butt nestled atop his thighs, Murphy released her waist and moved to her front for her bound hands. He lifted them and stretched her forward until the rope reached the hook welded to the bed frame.

With her bindings holding her stretched taut, she discovered that the position left her breasts dangling in Chase's face. A fact he acknowledged immediately by grasping a nipple between his teeth and biting down. A wicked burst of pain blended with the pleasure of her clit rubbing against his shaft.

Sweat broke out across her back, and Eve ground her teeth to keep things at bay. Already a new ball of fury began to build in her womb, leaving her no choice but to fight against it.

Before she could process the sensations Chase created, Murphy was behind her, prodding her backside with the head of his cock. He didn't warn her or give her time to consider what was about to happen. He pressed inside in one dark, merciless slide, opening her wide for his full length.

PLAY WITH ME

Fuck. She'd never been so full and stretched in her life. An intense myriad of sensations overwhelmed her. Her whimpers went unheeded, and every attempt to move was stopped by the grip both Chase and Murphy had on her.

A slight twinge of fear stole over her but was quickly forgotten the minute they began to move. One in, the other out, over and over again. The rhythm they worked her with played out like a beautiful instrument strung for her pleasure alone.

The heat from the friction they created threatened to burn her alive. Never before had she dreamed sex could be this delicious — this hedonistic.

"Jesus, Eve. So tight," Murphy exclaimed.

"Not to mention I can feel the head of your dick rubbing over me every time you move in her."

The muscles strained in Chase's neck. Evidence of how hard he worked to maintain control. "Come whenever you want, sweetheart, 'cause I doubt either one of us is going to last."

That one little word was all it took. Chase said come and Eve did. Bright lights flashed in her mind. A shining star exploding before her, rocking her world. Chase bit a nipple when she screamed, ensuring her flight didn't land. With both men riding her hard, she couldn't move. Bound and filled, she had no choice but to feel the ecstasy and enjoy the bliss.

On a fast thrust that touched every single nerve ending he could find, Murphy exclaimed, "You're mine."

"Mine too." Chase repeated the sentiment on a powerful push of his own.

The final missing piece of Eve locked into place. If someone had told her she'd fall in love with two dominating men who would show her that she was meant for submission, she'd have laughed in their face. Yet, here she was, completely and hopelessly in love. She stared into Chase's eyes, knowing he saw to her deepest, darkest soul, and climaxed again. This one solely for them in an ultimate display of surrender.

Her muscles clasped her masters and dragged them along for the ride. They gasped, groaned, and swore at her for stealing their control. They'd make her pay for that later, but for the moment all she felt was peace. The sweet calm after a long and rocky storm. The one thing she'd craved most and been unable to attain on her own. The path to which had been hidden in her desperate denial of submission.

She was finally home.

As the intensity of their lovemaking faded, she uttered the three final words: "I love you."

# # #

Thank you so much for reading! I hope you enjoyed reading *Play With Me, the first in my Pleasure Playground series,* as much as I enjoyed writing it. I'm hard at work writing my next romance, but while you are waiting I invite you to check out all the books I have available to read in the meantime. You can see the full list with links on the books page of my website at http://elizagayle.net

Book two in the Pleasure Playground series is *Power Play* and is also available now.

If you'd like to be notified when my next book comes out or when I run any contests, please sign up for my newsletter on my website.

POWER PLAY

BOOK 2: Pleasure Playground

NOW AVAILABLE

She wants the escape. He wants control. They both need love.

Jennifer Croft is at the peak of her career. As a bondage model at Altered Ego, she's become the crème de la crème of the fetish world, ensuring herself a top spot in her profession. The world is her oyster. Her personal life on the other hand... It's not pretty. Only her fascination with pain play keeps the ghosts of her past at bay.

After tragedy sends Daegan McKenna to the South for a much needed change of pace, the last thing he expects to find is a closet submissive hiding in plain sight. She's hot-tempered and in denial — a heady combination that brings out the dominant looking for a challenge. He's already loved and lost more than one man should, but the haunted look in her eyes prompts him to make her an offer. He'll indulge her darkest fantasies, if she'll agree to give up control. Then he'll let her go.

Unfortunately, the past never stays in the past and old insecurities cause complications neither of them wanted. Now temporary is not enough.

PAPERBACK BOOK PALACE
4106 18 AVE NW
ROCHESTER MN 55901
507-288-1218
www.ThePaperbackBookPalace.com

Made in the USA
Lexington, KY
14 September 2015